# WHY THE CHIMES RANG

All that the nearest of them saw was the childish figure of Little Brother.

# why the chimes rang

## and other stories

By
### RAYMOND MACDONALD ALDEN

*with illustrations by*
### EVELYN COPELMAN

### THE BOBBS-MERRILL COMPANY

*Indianapolis*  PUBLISHERS  *New York*

To

D. H. A.

# CONTENTS

# WHY THE CHIMES RANG

# Why the Chimes Rang

THERE was once, in a far-away country where few people have ever traveled, a wonderful church. It stood on a high hill in the midst of a great city; and every Sunday, as well as on sacred days like Christmas, thousands of people climbed the hill to its great archways, looking like lines of ants all moving in the same direction.

When you came to the building itself, you found stone columns and dark passages, and a grand entrance leading to the main room of the church. This room was so long that one standing at the doorway could scarcely see to the other end, where the choir stood by the marble altar. In the farthest corner was the organ; and this organ was so loud that sometimes when it played, the people for miles around would close their shutters and prepare for a great thunderstorm. Altogether, no such church as this was ever seen before, especially when it was lighted up for some festival, and crowded with people, young and old.

But the strangest thing about the whole building was the wonderful chime of bells. At one corner of the church was a great gray tower, with ivy growing over it as far up as one could see. I say as far as one could see because the tower was quite great enough to fit the great church, and it rose so far into the sky that it was only in very fair weather that anyone claimed to be able to see the top. Even then one could not be certain that it was in sight. Up and up and up climbed the stones and the ivy; and, as the men who built the church had been dead for hundreds of years, everyone had forgotten how high the tower was supposed to be.

Now, all the people knew that at the top of the tower was a chime of Christmas bells. They had hung there ever since the church had been built, and were the most beautiful bells in the world. Some thought it was because a great

12

musician had cast them and arranged them in their place; others said it was because of the great height, which reached up where the air was clearest and purest. However that might be, no one who had ever heard the chimes denied that they were the sweetest in the world. Some described them as sounding like angels far up in the sky; others, as sounding like strange winds singing through the trees.

But the fact was that no one had heard them for years and years. There was an old man living not far from the church who said that his mother had spoken of hearing them when she was a little girl, and he was the only one who was sure of as much as that. They were Christmas chimes, you see, and were not meant to be played by men or on common days. It was the custom on Christmas Eve for all the people to bring to the church their offerings to the Christ child; and when the greatest and best offering was laid on the altar, there used to come sounding through the music of the choir the Christmas chimes far up in the tower. Some said that the wind rang them, and others that they were so high the angels could set them swinging. But for many long years they had never been heard.

It was said that people had been growing less careful of their gifts for the Christ child, and that no offering was brought great enough to deserve the music of the chimes. Every Christmas Eve the rich people still crowded to the

13

altar, each one trying to bring some gift better than any other, without giving anything that he wanted for himself, and the church was crowded with those who thought that perhaps the wonderful bells might be heard again. But although the service was splendid and the offerings plenty, only the roar of the wind could be heard, far up in the stone tower.

Now, a number of miles from the city, in a little country village where nothing could be seen of the great church but glimpses of the tower when the weather was fine, lived a boy named Pedro and his little brother. They knew very little about the Christmas chimes, but they had heard of the service in the church on Christmas Eve, and had a secret plan, which they had often talked over when by themselves, to go see the beautiful celebration.

"Nobody can guess, Little Brother," Pedro would say, "all the fine things there are to see and hear; and I have even heard it said that the Christ child sometimes comes down to bless the service. What if we could see Him?"

The day before Christmas was bitterly cold, with a few lonely snowflakes flying in the air and a hard white crust on the ground. Sure enough, Pedro and Little Brother were able to slip quietly away early in the afternoon; and although the walking was hard in the frosty air, before nightfall they had trudged so far, hand in hand, that they saw the lights of the big city just ahead of them. Indeed, they were about to enter one of the great gates in the wall that surrounded it when they saw something dark on the snow near their path, and stepped aside to look at it.

It was a poor woman who had fallen just outside the city, too sick and tired to get in where she might have found shelter. The soft snow made of a drift a sort of pillow for her, and she would soon be so sound asleep in the wintry air that no one could ever waken her again. All this Pedro saw in a moment, and he knelt down beside her and tried to rouse her, even tugging at her arm a little, as though he would have tried to carry her away. He turned her face toward him so that he could rub some of the snow on it, and when he had looked at her silently a moment, he stood up again and said:

"It's no use, Little Brother. You will have to go on alone."

"Alone?" cried Little Brother. "And you not see the Christmas festival?"

"No," said Pedro, and he could not keep back a bit of a choking sound in his throat. "See this poor woman. Her face looks like the Madonna in the chapel window, and she will freeze to death if nobody cares for her. Everyone has gone to the church now, but when you come back you can bring someone to help her. I will rub her face to keep her from

15

freezing, and perhaps get her to eat the bun that is left in my pocket."

"But I cannot bear to leave you, and go on alone," said Little Brother.

"Both of us need not miss the service," said Pedro, "and it had better be I than you. You can easily find your way to the church; and you must see and hear everything twice, Little Brother—once for you and once for me. I am sure the Christ child must know how I should love to come with you and worship Him; and oh! if you get a chance, Little Brother, to slip up to the altar without getting in anyone's way, take this little silver piece of mine, and lay it down for my offering when no one is looking. Do not forget where you have left me, and forgive me for not going with you."

In this way he hurried Little Brother off to the city, and winked hard to keep back the tears as he heard the crunching footsteps sounding farther and farther away in the twilight. It was pretty hard to lose the music and splendor of the Christmas celebration that he had been planning for so long, and spend the time instead in that lonely place in the snow.

The great church was a wonderful place that night. Everyone said that it had never looked so bright and beautiful before. When the organ played and the thousands of people sang, the walls shook with the sound, and little Pedro, away outside the city wall, felt the earth tremble around him.

At the close of the service came the procession with the offerings to be laid on the altar. Rich men and great men marched proudly up to lay down their gifts to the Christ child. Some brought wonderful jewels, some baskets of gold so heavy that they could scarcely carry them down the aisle. A great writer laid down a book that he had been making for years and years. And last of all walked the king of the country, hoping with all the rest to win for himself the chime of the Christmas bells. There went a great murmur through the church, as the people saw the king take from his head the royal crown, all set with precious stones, and lay it gleaming on the altar, as his offering to the holy Child. "Surely," everyone said, "we shall hear the bells now, for nothing like this has ever happened before."

But still only the cold old wind was heard in the tower, and the people shook their heads; and some of them said, as they had before, that they never really believed the story of the chimes, and doubted if they ever rang at all.

The procession was over, and the choir began the closing hymn. Suddenly the organist stopped playing as though he had been shot, and everyone looked at the old minister, who was standing by the altar holding up his hand for

17

silence. Not a sound could be heard from anyone in the church, but as all the people strained their ears to listen, there came softly, but distinctly, swinging through the air, the sound of the chimes in the tower. So far away and yet so clear the music seemed—so much sweeter were the notes than anything that had been heard before, rising and falling away up there in the sky, that the people in the church sat for a moment as still as though something held each of them by the shoulders. Then they all stood up together and stared straight at the altar, to see what great gift had awakened the long-silent bells.

But all that the nearest of them saw was the childish figure of Little Brother, who had crept softly down the aisle when no one was looking, and had laid Pedro's little piece of silver on the altar.

# The Knights of the Silver Shield

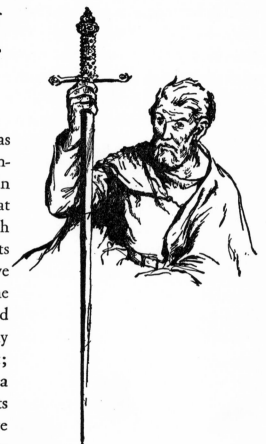

THERE was once a splendid castle in a forest, with great stone walls and a high gateway, and turrets that rose away above the tallest trees. The forest was dark and dangerous, and many cruel giants lived in it; but in the castle was a company of knights who were kept there by the king of the country, to help travelers who might be in the forest and to fight with the giants whenever they could.

Each of these knights wore a beautiful suit of armor and

carried a long spear, while over his helmet there floated a great red plume that could be seen a long way off by anyone in distress. But the most wonderful thing about the knights' armor was their shields. They were not like those of other knights, but had been made by a great magician who had lived in the castle many years before. They were made of silver, and sometimes shone in the sunlight with dazzling brightness; but at other times the surface of the shields would be clouded as though by a mist, and one could not see his face reflected there as he could when they shone brightly.

Now, when each young knight received his spurs and his armor, a new shield was also given him from among those that the magician had made; and when the shield was new its surface was always cloudy and dull. But as the knight began to do service against the giants, or went on expeditions to help poor travelers in the forest, his shield grew brighter and brighter, so that he could see his face clearly reflected in it. But if he proved to be a lazy or cowardly knight, and let the giants get the better of him, or did not care what became of the travelers, then the shield grew more and more cloudy, until the knight became ashamed to carry it.

But this was not all. When any one of the knights fought a particularly hard battle and won the victory, or when he went on some hard errand for the lord of the castle and was successful, not only did his silver shield grow brighter, but when one looked into the center of it he could see something like a golden star shining in its very heart. This was the greatest honor that a knight could achieve, and the other knights always spoke of such a one as having "won his star." It was usually not till he was pretty old and tried as a soldier that he could win it. At the time when this story begins, the lord of the castle himself was the only one of the knights whose shield bore the golden star.

There came a time when the worst of the giants in the forest gathered themselves together to have a battle against the knights. They made a camp in a dark hollow not far from the castle, and gathered all their best warriors together, and all the knights made ready to fight them. The windows of the castle were closed and barred; the air was full of the noise of armor being made ready for use; and the knights were so excited that they could scarcely rest or eat.

Now there was a young knight in the castle named Sir Roland, who was among those most eager for the battle. He was a splendid warrior, with eyes that shone like stars whenever there was anything to do in the way of knightly deeds. And although he was still quite young, his shield

21

had begun to shine enough to show plainly that he had done bravely in some of his errands through the forest. This battle, he thought, would be the great opportunity of his life. And on the morning of the day when they were to go forth to it, and all the knights assembled in the great hall of the castle to receive the commands of their leaders, Sir Roland hoped that he would be put in the most dangerous place of all, so that he could show what knightly stuff he was made of.

But when the lord of the castle came to him, as he went about in full armor giving his commands, he said: "One brave knight must stay behind and guard the gateway of the castle, and it is you, Sir Roland, being one of the youngest, whom I have chosen for this."

At these words Sir Roland was so disappointed that he bit his lip and closed his helmet over his face so that the other knights might not see it. For a moment he felt as if he must reply angrily to the commander, and tell him that it was not right to leave so sturdy a knight behind when he was eager to fight. But he struggled against this feeling, and went quietly to look after his duties at the gate. The gateway was high and narrow, and was reached from outside by a high, narrow bridge that crossed the moat, which surrounded the castle on every side. When an enemy approached, the knight on guard rang a great bell just inside the gate, and the bridge was drawn up against the castle wall so that no one could come across the moat. So the giants had long ago given up trying to attack the castle itself.

Today the battle was to be in the dark hollow in the forest, and it was not likely that there would be anything to do at the castle gate except to watch it like a common doorkeeper. It was not strange that Sir Roland thought someone else might have done this.

Presently all the other knights marched out in their flashing armor, their red plumes waving over their heads, and their spears in their hands. The lord of the castle stopped only to tell Sir Roland to keep guard over the gate until they had all returned, and to let no one enter. Then they went into the shadows of the forest and were soon lost to sight.

Sir Roland stood looking after them long after they had gone, thinking how happy he would be if he were on the way to battle like them. But after a little he put this out of his mind and tried to think of pleasanter things. It was a long time before anything happened, or any word came from the battle.

At last Sir Roland saw one of the knights come limping down the path to the castle, and he went out on the bridge to meet him. Now, this knight was not a brave one, and he had been frighened away as soon as he was wounded.

"I have been hurt," he said, "so that I cannot fight any more. But I could watch the gate for you if you would like to go back in my place."

At first Sir Roland's heart leaped with joy at this, but then he remembered what the commander had told him on going away, and he said:

"I should like to go, but a knight belongs where his commander has put him. My place is here at the gate, and I cannot open it even for you. Your place is at the battle."

The knight was ashamed when he heard this, and he presently turned about and went into the forest again.

So Sir Roland kept guard silently for another hour. Then there came an old beggar woman down the path to the castle, and asked Sir Roland if she might come in and have some food. He told her that no one could enter the castle that day, but that he would send a servant out to her with food, and that she might sit and rest as long as she would.

"I have been past the hollow in the forest where the battle is going on," said the old woman while she was waiting for her food.

"And how do you think it is going?" asked Sir Roland.

"Badly for the knights, I am afraid," said the old woman. "The giants are fighting as they have never fought before. I should think you had better go and help your friends."

"The Shield! The Shield! Sir Roland's Shield!"

"I should like to, indeed," said Sir Roland. "But I am set to guard the gateway of the castle, and cannot leave."

"One fresh knight would make a great difference when they are all weary with fighting," said the old woman. "I should think that, while there are no enemies about, you would be much more useful there."

"You may well think so," said Sir Roland, "and so may I; but it is neither you nor I that is commander here."

"I suppose," said the old woman then, "that you are one of the kind of knights who like to keep out of fighting. You are lucky to have so good an excuse for staying at home." And she laughed a thin and taunting laugh.

Then Sir Roland was very angry, and thought that if it were only a man instead of a woman, he would show him whether he liked fighting or no. But as it was a woman, he shut his lips and set his teeth hard together, and as the servant came just then with the food he had sent for, he gave it to the old woman quickly, and shut the gate that she might not talk to him any more.

It was not very long before he heard someone calling outside. Sir Roland opened the gate and saw standing at the other end of the drawbridge a little old man in a long black cloak. "Why are you knocking here?" he said. "The castle is closed today."

"Are you Sir Roland?" said the little old man.

"Yes," said Sir Roland.

"Then you ought not to be staying here when your commander and his knights are having so hard a struggle with the giants, and when you have the chance to make of yourself the greatest knight in this kingdom. Listen to me! I have brought you a magic sword."

As he said this, the old man drew from under his coat a wonderful sword that flashed in the sunlight as if it were covered with diamonds. "This is the sword of all swords," he said, "and it is for you, if you will leave your idling here by the castle gate and carry it to the battle. Nothing can stand before it. When you lift it the giants will fall back, your master will be saved, and you will be crowned the victorious knight—the one who will soon take his commander's place as lord of the castle."

Now Sir Roland believed that it was a magician who was speaking to him, for it certainly appeared to be a magic sword. It seemed so wonderful that the sword should be brought to him that he reached out his hand as though he would take it, and the little old man came forward as though he would cross the drawbridge into the castle. But as he did so, it came to Sir Roland's mind again that that bridge and the gateway had been intrusted to him, and he called out "No!" to the old man, so that he stopped where he was standing. But he waved the shining sword in the

26

air again and said: "It is for you! Take it and win the victory!"

Sir Roland was really afraid that if he looked any longer at the sword, or listened to any more words of the old man, he would not be able to hold himself within the castle. For this reason he struck the great bell at the gateway, which was the signal for the servants inside to pull in the chains of the drawbridge, and instantly they began to pull, and the drawbridge came up, so that the old man could not cross it to enter the castle, nor Sir Roland to go out.

Then, as he looked across the moat, Sir Roland saw a wonderful thing. The little old man threw off his black cloak, and as he did so he began to grow bigger and bigger, until in a minute more he was a giant as tall as any in the forest. At first Sir Roland could scarcely believe his eyes. Then he realized that this must be one of their giant enemies, who had changed himself to a little old man through some magic power, that he might make his way into the castle while all the knights were away. Sir Roland shuddered to think what might have happened if he had taken the sword and left the gate unguarded. The giant shook his fist across the moat that lay between them, and then, knowing that he could do nothing more, he went angrily back into the forest.

Sir Roland now resolved not to open the gate again, and

27

to pay no attention to any other visitor. But it was not long before he heard a sound that made him spring forward in joy. It was the bugle of the lord of the castle, and there came sounding after it the bugles of many of the knights that were with him, pealing so joyfully that Sir Roland was sure they were safe and happy. As they came nearer, he could hear their shouts of victory. So he gave the signal to let down the drawbridge again, and went out to meet them. They were dusty and bloodstained and weary, but they had won the battle with the giants; and it had been such a great victory that there had never been a happier home-coming.

Sir Roland greeted them all as they passed in over the bridge, and then, when he had closed the gate and fastened it, he followed them into the great hall of the castle. The lord of the castle took his place on the highest seat, with the other knights about him, and Sir Roland came forward with the key of the gate to give his account of what he had done in the place to which the commander had appointed him. The lord of the castle bowed to him as a sign for him to begin, but just as he opened his mouth to speak, one of the knights cried out:

"The shield! The shield! Sir Roland's shield!"

Everyone turned and looked at the shield which Sir Roland carried on his left arm. He himself could see only the top of it, and did not know what they could mean. But what they saw was the golden star of knighthood, shining brightly from the center of Sir Roland's shield. There had never been such amazement in the castle before.

Sir Roland knelt before the lord of the castle to receive his commands. He still did not know why everyone was looking at him so excitedly, and wondered if he had in some way done wrong.

"Speak, Sir Knight," said the commander, as soon as he could find his voice after his surprise, "and tell us all that has happened today at the castle. Have you been attacked? Have any giants come hither? Did you fight them alone?"

"No, my Lord," said Sir Roland. "Only one giant has been here, and he went away silently when he found he could not enter."

Then he told all that had happened through the day.

When he had finished, the knights all looked at one another, but no one spoke a word. Then they looked again at Sir Roland's shield to make sure that their eyes had not deceived them, and there the golden star was still shining.

After a little silence the lord of the castle spoke.

"Men make mistakes," he said, "but our silver shields are never mistaken. Sir Roland has fought and won the hardest battle of all today."

Then the others all rose and saluted Sir Roland, who was the youngest knight that ever carried the golden star.

# The Boy Who Discovered the Spring

THERE came once a little Elf Boy to live on this earth, and he was so much pleased with it that he stayed, never caring to go back to his own world. I do not know where his own world was, or just how he came to leave it. Some thought that he was dropped by accident from some falling star, and some that he had flown away, thinking that he could fly back again whenever he chose, because he did not know that children always lose their wings when they come into this world. But no one knew certainly, as he never told anyone; and, after all, it did not matter, since, as I have already said, he liked the earth so much that he did not care to leave it.

There was a Hermit who lived in the valley where the little Boy had first come, and, as he had a room in his house for a visitor, he took him in, and they grew to like each other so well that again the little Boy did not care to go away, nor did the Hermit care to have him. The Hermit had not always been a hermit, but he had become a sorrowful man, and did not care to live where other people lived or to share any of their pleasures. The reason he had become a sorrowful man was that his only child had died, and it seemed to him that there was nothing worth living for after that. So he moved to the lonely valley, and I suppose would have spent the rest of his life by himself if it had not been for the little Elf Boy.

It was a very lovely valley, with great, green meadows that sloped down to a rippling brook, and in summertime were full of red and white and yellow blossoms. Over the brook there hung green trees, whose roots made pleasant places to rest when one was tired; and along the water's edge there grew blue flowers, while many little frogs and other live creatures played there. It was summertime when the little Elf Boy came, and the flowers and the trees and

31

the brook and the frogs made him very happy. I think that in the world from which he came they did not have such things: it was made chiefly of gold and silver and precious stones, instead of things that grow and blossom and keep one company. So the Elf Boy was very happy. He did not ask to go to play in the village over the hill, but was quite content with the meadows and the brook-side. The only thing that did not please him was that the old Hermit still remained sorrowful, thinking always of his child who had died; and this the Elf Boy did not understand, for in the world from which he came nothing ever died, and he thought it strange that if the Hermit's child had died he did not patiently wait for him to come back again.

So the summer went merrily on, and the Elf Boy learned to know the names of all the flowers in the meadow, and to love them dearly. He also became so well acquainted with the birds that they would come to him for crumbs, and sit on the branches close by to sing to him; the frogs would do the same thing, and although the Elf Boy did not think their voices as sweet as those of the birds, he was too polite to let them know it.

But when September came, there began to be a sad change. The first thing the Elf Boy noticed was that the birds began to disappear from the meadows. When he complained of this, the Hermit told him they had gone to

32

When the music began, a strange thing happened. The hermit sang the Easter
song with the others.

make their visit to the Southland, and would come back again; and this he easily believed. But as time went on, and the air became more and more still as the last of them took their flight, he began to lose heart.

What was worse, at the same time the flowers began to disappear from the meadows. They were dead, the Hermit said, and in this way the Elf Boy learned what that meant. At first others came to take their places, and he tried to learn to like the flowers of autumn as well as those which he had known first. But as these faded and dropped off, none came after them. The mornings grew colder, and the leaves on the trees were changing in a strange way. When they grew red and yellow, instead of green, the Elf Boy thought it was a queer thing for them to put on different colors, and wondered how long it would last. But when they began to fall, he was very sad indeed. At last there came a day when every limb was bare, except for a few dried leaves at the top of one of the tallest trees. The Elf Boy was almost broken-hearted.

One morning he went out early to see what new and dreadful thing had happened in the night, for it seemed now that every night took something beautiful out of the world. He made his way toward the brook, but when he reached the place where he usually heard it calling to him as it ran merrily over the stones, he could not hear a

33

sound. He stopped and listened, but everything was wonderfully still. Then he ran as fast as his feet would carry him to the border of the brook. Sure enough, it had stopped running. It was covered with a hard sheet of ice.

The Elf Boy turned and went to the Hermit's house. By the time he had reached it, the tears were running down his cheeks.

"Why, what is the matter?" asked the Hermit.

"The brook is dead," said the Elf Boy.

"I think not," said the Hermit. "It is frozen over, but that will not hurt it. Be patient, and it will sing to you again."

"No," said the Elf Boy. "You told me that the birds would come back, and they have not come. You told me that the trees were not dead, but their leaves have every one gone, and I am sure they are. You told me that the flowers had seeds that did not die, but would make other flowers; but I cannot find them, and the meadow is bare and dark. Even the grass is not green any more. It is a dead world. In the summertime I did not see how you could be sorrowful; but now I do not see how anyone can be happy."

The Hermit thought it would be of no use to try to explain anything more to the Elf Boy; so he said again, "Be patient," and tried to find some books in which he could teach the Boy to read, and make him forget the outside world.

The next time they went for a walk to the village over the hill, the Elf Boy was very curious to see whether the same thing had happened there that had happened in their valley. Of course it had: the trees there seemed dead, too, and the flowers were all gone from the door-yards. The Boy expected that everyone in the village would now be as sorrowful as the Hermit, and he was very much surprised when he saw them looking as cheerful as ever. There were some boys playing on the street corner who seemed to be as happy as boys could be. One of them spoke to the Elf Boy, and he answered:

"How can you play so happily when such a dreadful thing has happened to the world?"

"Why, what has happened?"

"The flowers and trees are dead," said the Elf Boy, "and the birds are gone, and the brook is frozen, and the meadow is bare and gray. And it is so on this side of the hill also."

Then the boys in the street laughed merrily, and did not answer the Elf Boy, for they remembered that he was a stranger in the world, and supposed he would not understand if they should try to talk to him. And he went on through the village, not daring to speak to any others, but

35

all the time wondering that the people could still be so happy.

As the winter came on, the Hermit taught him many things from the books in his house, and the Elf Boy grew interested in them and was not always sad. When the snow came he found ways to play in it, and even saw that the meadow was beautiful again, though in a different way from what it had been in summer. Yet still he could not think the world by any means so pleasant a place as it had been in the time of flowers and birds; and if it were not that he had become very fond of the Hermit, who was now the only friend he could remember, he would have wished to go back to the world from which he had come. It seemed to him now that the Hermit must miss him very much if he should go away, since they two were the only people who seemed really to understand how sorrowful a place the earth is.

So the weeks went by. One day in March, as he and the Hermit sat at their books, drops of water began to fall from the eaves of the roof, and they saw that the snow was melting in the sunshine.

"Do you want to take a little walk down toward the brook?" asked the Hermit. "I should not wonder if I could prove to you today that it has not forgotten how to talk to you."

36

"Yes," said the Elf Boy, though he did not think the Hermit could be right. It was months since he had cared to visit the brook, it made him so sad to find it still and cold.

When they reached the foot of the hillside the sheet of ice was still there, as he had expected.

"Never mind," said the Hermit. "Come out on the ice with me and put down your ear and listen."

So the Elf Boy put down his ear and listened; and he heard, as plainly as though there were no ice between, the voice of the brook gurgling in the bottom of its bed. He clapped his hands for joy.

"It is waking up, you see," said the Hermit. "Other things will waken too, if you will be patient."

The Elf Boy did not know quite what to think, but he waited day after day with his eyes and ears wide open to see if anything else might happen; and wonderful things did happen all the time. The brook sang more and more distinctly, and at last broke through its cold coverlet and went dancing along in full sight. One morning, while the snow was still around the house, the Elf Boy heard a chirping sound, and, looking from his window, saw a red robin outside asking for his breakfast.

"Why," cried the Boy, "have you really come back again?"

37

"Certainly," said the robin, "don't you know it is almost spring?"

But the Elf Boy did not understand what he said.

There was a pussy willow growing by the brook, and the Boy's next discovery was that hundreds of little gray buds were coming out. He watched them grow bigger from day to day, and while he was doing this the snow was melting away in great patches where the sun shone warmest on the meadow, and the blades of grass that came up into the daylight were greener than anything the Elf Boy had ever seen.

Then the pink buds came on the maple trees, and unfolded day by day. And the fruit trees in the Hermit's orchard were as white with blossoms as they had lately been with snow.

"Not a single tree is dead," said the Elf Boy.

Last of all came the wild flowers—blue and white violets near the brook, dandelions around the house, and, a little later, yellow buttercups all over the meadow. Slowly but steadily the world was made over, until it glowed with white and green and gold.

The Elf Boy was wild with joy. One by one his old friends came back, and he could not bear to stay in the house for many minutes from morning to night. Now he knew what the wise Hermit had meant by saying, "Be pa-

38

tient"; and he began to wonder again that the Hermit could be sorrowful in so beautiful a world.

One morning the church bells in the village—whose ringing was the only sound that ever came from the village over the hill—rang so much longer and more joyfully than usual that the Elf Boy asked the Hermit why they did so. The Hermit looked in one of his books and answered:

"It is Easter Day. The village people celebrate it on one Sunday every spring."

"May we not go also?" asked the Elf Boy, and as it was the first time he had ever asked to go to the village, the Hermit could not refuse to take him.

The village was glowing with flowers. There were many fruit trees, and they, too, were in blossom. Everyone who passed along the street seemed either to wear flowers or to carry them in his hand. The people were all entering the churchyard; and here the graves, which had looked so gray and cold when the Hermit and the Boy had last seen them, were beautiful with flowers that the village people had planted or had strewn over them for Easter.

The people all passed into the church. But the Hermit and the Elf Boy, who never went where there was a crowd, stayed outside where the hummingbirds and bees were flying happily among the flowers. Suddenly there came from the church a burst of music. To the Elf Boy it seemed the most beautiful sound he had ever heard. He put his finger on his lip to show the Hermit that he wanted to listen. These were the words they sang:

*"I am He that liveth, and was dead; and, behold, I am alive for evermore!"*

The Boy took hold of the Hermit's hand and led him to the church door, that they might hear still better. He was very happy.

"Oh," he cried, "I do not believe that anything ever really dies."

The Hermit looked down at him and smiled. "Perhaps not," he said.

When the music began again, a strange thing happened. The Hermit sang the Easter song with the others. It was the first time he had sung for many years.

# The Brook in the King's Garden

THERE was once a King of a far-away country who was a tyrant. He did not care to make the people happy, but only to please himself. He was used to being obeyed so quickly by those who feared him, that he became very angry if anyone failed to do as he commanded. It seemed to him that not only people should obey him, but animals and plants and everything in the country where he ruled.

When he was walking in his garden, if he saw a plant or a tree that he did not like, he would wave his scepter at it and say "Be gone!" And when he next passed that way, it would be gone, for the King's servants, knowing how angry it made him to be disobeyed, would quickly remove anything that displeased him. In this way the King came

41

to think that even the wild things of nature were under his control.

There was a Brook that flowed through one side of the King's garden, after it had come down from a high mountain and passed through a meadow and along one side of the town. It was a merry, chattering Brook, that made almost anyone happy to hear it, and along its banks grew lovely willow trees and many fine flowers. In the palace garden, of course, were the loveliest flowers of all; and the King was very fond of walking along the margin of the Brook.

But one day while he was walking there, his foot slipped a little so that he stepped into the water; and as the water was cold, and he had on very good clothes which it might harm, the King grew very angry. He struck the Brook with his scepter, and it splashed the water into his face. This, of course, angered him all the more, and it seemed to him now that the Brook was laughing at him as it gurgled over the stones. So the King lifted up his scepter again and said: "Be gone! I will not have any Brook in my kingdom!"

When his officers heard this they were very much troubled. For they knew that the Brook would not obey the King, and they did not know how to make believe that it had. They could not hide it or take it away. No one knew just where it came from, so they could not stop it at the source; and if they did so, they knew that it would make a great deal of trouble in the town and in the country near by. For the Brook not only gave people pleasure by its music and its flowers, but it turned mill-wheels, and made ponds where people fished, and furnished water for people to drink, and made gardens and farms fertile, and did many useful things. So the officers decided that they would try to keep the King away from that part of the garden, hoping that he would forget what he had said.

But he did not forget. When he went out next day and saw the Brook flowing along as merrily as ever, singing over the stones, he said: "Why is the Brook not gone?" When his officers told him that the Brook would not obey him, he said: "It must obey me. Send for all my servants."

So they sent for all his servants, and the King said to them: "The Brook is a bad brook; I will not have it here. Take it away."

So the servants got pails and jars of every kind and began emptying the Brook. But although they worked for a great many hours, and filled all the tanks in the palace, and poured the water all over the garden, the Brook seemed to be as full as ever.

Then the King said: "Burn it up!" And they brought torches, and sheets of cotton dipped in oil, so as to make the brightest and hottest flames, and they threw these into

43

the Brook. But the Brook only laughed as the flames hissed in it, and it carried off the black shreds of the burnt cotton, and put out all the fire without seeming to work any harder than usual, and in a short time was flowing along as clean and bright as ever.

Then the King said: "Bury it!" And the servants brought carts full of dirt, such as they used in making embankments around the palace, and began to dump these into the Brook. At last it seemed that the King's will was going to be obeyed, for the Brook began to disappear in the great mass of dirt that was poured over it. The servants carried the dirt farther and farther up the stream, until at last they had choked it up at the point where it flowed into the palace grounds. The King thought now that it was gone altogether, and went into his palace contented.

Now the King had a little daughter whom he loved very much; and when she learned what had been done to the Brook, she felt so sorry that she nearly cried. For the Brook was one of her dearest friends, and she knew how much she would miss it. She lay awake for as much as an hour that night, thinking about it, and decided that in the morning she would go to the Good Gray Woman, and ask her what could be done.

The Good Gray Woman lived in a hut just outside the palace wall, and there was a tiny gate leading through the

44

wall from her house, which had been made so that people from the palace could go to see her; for she was very wise, and knew the water sprites and the flower sprites and all the other creatures that most people never see, and she was always ready to help anyone in trouble.

So, very early in the morning the little Princess knocked at the Good Gray Woman's door, and when it opened she told her friend about the Brook. "I am sure my father would not have done it," she said, "if he had known how good the Brook was, and how much we all thought of it. Will you not go to him and tell him about it? He will believe you."

The Good Gray Woman thought a minute. Then she said:

"I will not go myself, for I do not think I could tell the King anything that you cannot tell him just as well. But I will send some friends of mine instead, who I am quite sure can make him understand. What time does the King take his seat on the throne to hear those who have anything to say to him?"

"At nine o'clock every morning," said the Princess.

"Very well," said the Good Gray Woman. "If you are there at nine o'clock, you will see my friends there, too."

The Princess could not think what friends the Good

Gray Woman would send; but she believed her, and returned to the palace.

At nine o'clock the King took his seat on his throne and asked whether anyone had come to see him. The Princess was close at hand, waiting to see what would happen. As soon as the King had spoken, she saw in front of the throne two little winged creatures that seemed to have come there by magic, for no one had seen them enter the room. They hung in the air before the King like butterflies. One of them was gray, like a bit of floating mist, but it was also streaked with all the colors of the rainbow. The other was of a deep blue color that was almost green when the sun shone on it.

"We are water sprites," said these little creatures to the King, "and we have come to see your Majesty on important business."

"Very good," said the King. He had never seen such creatures before, and found them very interesting.

"I," said the first sprite, "belong to a waterdrop from a cloud that was hanging over your garden this morning, and I was also in the beautiful rainbow that your Majesty was admiring yesterday. I came to speak to you about the Brook."

"About the Brook?" said the King. "What do you know about it?"

"Why, I used to live in it," said the sprite. "Then I went on down to the ocean, and then the sun carried me up to the cloud country. And the cloud that I now belong to was all ready to give your garden a little shower this morning when we saw that the Brook was not there. This made all the drops that used to belong to the Brook feel very bad, for we hoped to get back to it again. So I came to ask you about it."

"Dear me!" said the King. "I had no idea that the Brook had anything to do with you. I shall have to think about it. And who are you?" he said to the other sprite.

"I belong to a waterdrop from the ocean," said the sprite. "I, too, once lived in the Brook, and have been waiting all night for the other drops that it always brings us. But they stopped coming, and we all felt very sorry. So I was sent to see what was the matter."

"Dear me!" said the King again. "I had no idea that the Brook had anything to do with you. I shall have to think about it. But you will have to come and see me some other time."

This was what the King always said when he did not feel sure whether he wanted to do what people were asking him to. When the sprites saw that he would say nothing more, they flew away as silently as they had come.

The Princess waited all day, hoping that her father

would think about what the sprites had told him, and command the Brook to be brought back again, for the sake of the clouddrops and the oceandrops. But the fact was he soon forgot all about it, and did nothing at all. So the Princess went again to the Good Gray Woman, and asked her if she could send any other friends to help her.

"Oh, yes," said the Good Gray Woman. "They will come tomorrow at the same time."

So the next morning when the King took his seat on his throne as usual and asked if anyone wished to see him, there were two more sprites hovering in the air before him. One of these was gray like a pebblestone, and the other looked as though it were covered with dark brown velvet, like a caterpillar.

"And who are you?" said the King.

"We are earth sprites," said the first one. "I belong to the little stones in your Majesty's garden. We were all being polished very beautifully by the Brook, and made ready for all sorts of pretty things. But now we are covered with dirt, and we cannot hear the Brook singing above us; so we have come to ask if it cannot come back again."

"Humph!" said the King. "More friends of the Brook, are you?"

"Yes," said the second sprite. "I belong to the rich, dark soil that lies around the roots of the trees in your Majesty's

48

If he saw a plant or tree that he did not like, he would wave his scepter at it, and say, "Be gone!"

garden. The Brook watered us every day, so that we could feed all the growing things that need us. But now we are getting dry and hard, the roots complain that we do not care for them as we used to; and we do not know what to do."

"It is very strange how much that Brook was doing," said the King. "We shall have to see about this. Perhaps we can get another Brook. Come and see me some other time."

So the little Princess again hoped that the King would now remember the Brook and have it brought back. But all that he did was to tell the gardener to take better care of the trees, for he heard that they were complaining of the dry season; and then he forgot all about it. The Princess hardly dared hope that the Good Gray Woman would have any other friends to send to help her, but she tried once again.

"Oh, yes," said the Good Gray Woman, "there are plenty more."

So the next morning, sure enough, there were two more sprites when the King sat down on his throne. These were the most beautiful of all. One of them had wings like the petals of a violet, and a body like a yellow crocus. The other was all in green.

"I don't want to see any more sprites," said the King,

49

"unless they have something new to talk about." But he did not know just how to send them away; so he was obliged to listen when they spoke.

"I am a flower sprite," said the first one, "and have always lived in your Majesty's garden, by the edge of the Brook. We thought you were very fond of us, and came to tell you that, now the Brook has gone, we are fast withering; and no new flowers will come up until it returns."

"And I," said the other sprite, "belong to the grass that grew at the edge of the Brook, and have come to tell you that all the grasses are missing it so much that we think you will surely have pity on us."

The King would not answer these sprites, because he was tired of making them all the same answer, and really did not know what to say. But when they had flown off, he said to himself:

"I cannot be bothered with so many sprites. If they keep coming I shall have nothing else to do but hear about the Brook and its friends. I wish it had never been buried."

Now this was just what the Princess was waiting for. She clapped her hands, crying:

"Then can we not have it back again?"

"I don't know how we could get it back," said the King. "But if you wish, you may ask the Good Gray Woman what we had better do."

50

The Princess ran off at once to do as the King said. When the Good Gray Woman heard about it she answered:

"Tell the King, your father, to go walking with you on the palace wall, and he will see what has become of the Brook."

So the Princess took the King by the hand, and they went walking on the top of the palace wall. When they came to the place where the Brook had flowed under the wall, they saw a very strange thing. The Brook had not been buried at all! When its channel in the palace garden had been choked with the dirt put there by the King's servants, it had simply turned aside and made another channel outside the wall; and there it was, flowing along as merrily as ever. Already some little flowers had sprung up along its new banks, and the grass was green all about it. Many children from the town were playing there, feeling very thankful that, instead of flowing into the King's garden, the Brook was out in the big free garden where they could all enjoy it.

When the King had seen all this, he called his servants and told them to take out all the dirt they had put into the Brook's channel when they had tried to bury it. And they did so. But the Brook liked its new channel very well; so, although it sent a little branch to flow in the old place

51

through the King's garden, carrying water to the flowers and trees that had missed it, it never really came back, but went on flowing in the place where it had found so many new friends. It soon made a path to the sea, and continued to send its drops to help make the ocean and the clouds and the rainbows, as well as to polish the stones and water the flowers along its banks. And although I have heard nothing of it for a long time, I am quite sure that it is flowing there merrily still.

# The Hunt for the Beautiful

THERE was once a boy named Karl who lived in a little village in a valley, far from all the great cities. It was a simple and quiet village, but very pleasant to see, because of the many flowers that grew in the people's gardens, and of the beautiful hills that lay just behind it. In the middle of the village was an old chapel, and as the boy's father was the sexton, their little house and garden were next door. The chapel was a dim, restful place, with stained-glass windows, which had been made hundreds of years before and had figures of saints and angels shimmering in them. Very often, when Karl was tired of both work and play, he would go in and sit there, and would sometimes fall asleep looking at the lovely pictures in the windows.

There was a particular reason why he was so much interested in the pictures, and that was that he wished to be a great artist. Before he had been old enough to read, he had drawn pictures wherever he could find a place to put them, and nothing made him so happy as to have a present of colored crayons or paints. Then, as he grew older, whatever money he could save for himself—which was not much, for his father and mother were poor—he spent in paying for lessons in drawing and painting from whoever could be found to teach him in the village.

But as the village was so small, Karl wished very much to go to see the world and to study painting with great teachers. The village people thought that he was already a wonderful painter, because he could sit down before a flower, or a house, or even a child's face, and make a copy of it so good that no one could think how it might be better. They could not see, therefore, why Karl was not satisfied. But he always told them that there were better pictures in the world than either he or they had ever seen, and that if they could once see them, they would never again be pleased with his.

"Well, in that case," the people answered, "why should we want to see them? If what you say is true, we should be less happy than we are now. We are pleased with your pictures, and you should be pleased with them, too."

"No," said Karl. "I cannot be pleased with anything until it is the very best I can do, and I believe I can do still better. If I could only see the most beautiful things in the world, I could paint them, at any rate. I have painted everything in this place,—the old chapel, and the hills behind the village, and the flowers in our garden, and the prettiest children. But all the time I have known that these are not the most beautiful sights. Somewhere is the most beautiful sight in the world. I shall never be happy till I have seen it."

So they could not make him believe that they were right, and, although he enjoyed his work, he was never pleased with it when it was done. At last there came a time when he thought he could go away to see the world. His brothers were now old enough to be of help to his father; and his mother, though she would be very lonely without him, seemed almost as eager as he was that he should make his great journey. So one morning, he bade them all good-by and started down the road that led into the big world.

There was really no one but Karl himself who knew why it was that he felt so sure he must go away. Something had happened more than a year before which he had kept secret but had never forgotten. One day he had been work-

55

ing hard at a picture, as he always did in his spare minutes, and had grown tired and discouraged because when it was finished it was not as beautiful as he had hoped. So he had gone into the little old chapel to rest and comfort himself, as I have said that he did so often.

There was one window in the chapel that Karl had always thought especially beautiful. In it was the figure of a great white angel, whom he always called the Angel of Beauty, not knowing what her real name might be. He knelt under the window, where he could look up into the face of this Angel, and thought how fine it would be if she could only speak to him, and give him a message, as the angels and saints had done in earlier times.

"I know what I would say to her," he said to himself. "I would ask her: When can I ever paint the beautiful picture that I am always trying to?"

Then a very wonderful thing happened. Karl had asked this question aloud, because he was so much in earnest about it and knew that no one else was in the chapel to hear him. Now, as he looked at the face of the Angel in the window, he suddenly saw her lips open; and then, before he realized what it could mean, she was speaking to him. This was what he heard:

"When you have seen the most beautiful sight in the world."

56

That was all. Karl asked more questions, and begged the Angel to tell him how he could find the most beautiful sight, but she never spoke to him again, though sometimes afterward, when he would go to the little chapel to rest after a hard day's work, he would think that he saw her lips breaking into a kindly smile as she looked down upon him in the dim light. He never told anyone, not even his father and mother, of the words that she had spoken to him, but he never ceased to think of them; and this was why he was so eager to set out on his journey, as we have seen that he did at last.

It would take a very long time to tell about all of Karl's travels, during the months that followed his going away from home. On the whole, though he saw many fine sights and made new friends, it was a wearisome journey. He did not have money enough to travel in comfort, and sometimes he would find that he had spent everything he had, and would be obliged to stop somewhere for a few weeks until he could earn enough to take him farther. Sometimes he would walk many miles, from one city to another, and arrive there with his feet so sore and his back so tired and aching that it seemed to him he wanted only one thing— his little bed in his little room in the old home.

But all this would not have mattered, if only he could have found the thing for which he had set out. It always

57

seemed to be just a little distance ahead of him. At first he thought that he would be most likely to find it in the galleries where the paintings and statues of all the greatest artists were collected. So he visited these in the different cities, and once or twice he found a painting or a statue so wonderfully beautiful that he exclaimed: "Surely this is the most beautiful thing in the world!" But always someone said to him: "No; wait till you have seen such-and-such a picture in such-and-such a gallery. That is without doubt more beautiful than this." So he would go on hopefully to the other gallery, but always with the same uncertainty as to whether he had found what he was searching for.

After many weeks spent in this way, Karl decided that it was not in pictures or statues, but in beautiful scenes of nature, that he was most likely to find what he sought. For whenever he saw a lovely picture of a lake or a mountain or a valley, it would occur to him that if the picture were so beautiful, the landscape itself must be still more so. So, as the summer was now coming on, he visited the loveliest countries that he could hear of, where the mountains were covered with snow the year round, but the valleys between were filled with wonderful flowers, and brooks went singing down the slopes and emptied themselves into lakes as blue as the sky. He had never dreamed of anything

58

so beautiful as some of these places, yet the same thing happened that had happened before. Whenever he would say to another traveler that he thought this must be the most beautiful sight in the world, the traveler would say: "No. I have seen one still better; you will find it in the Valley of So-and-so." So Karl would take up his journey again, always with new hope.

Meantime he did not get good news from home. His mother wrote him that his father was dead, and this made him very sad. Then she wrote that it had been a hard winter in their neighborhood, so that his brothers had found it difficult to earn as much as usual, and they had had to sell some of their land to buy fuel to keep them warm. But she did not ask Karl to come home, for she was as anxious as he was that he should become a great artist, and was sure that he would succeed if he only had good luck on his journey. So she told him to go on, and not to be troubled about the things that were happening at home, for she would not have written of them at all if it had not been to explain why she could not send him any money.

So Karl continued his journey a little farther, and tried to keep a good heart. At last he felt more certain than ever before that he was going to find the object of his search, for a number of travelers had told him that he ought to go to see a certain castle on a certain mountain, in a certain

59

distant country, where the view was undoubtedly the most beautiful in the world. So many people told him this that Karl felt now that all he had to do was to get money enough to take him to that country, when his journey would be ended; but this was hard to do. So he stopped in the city where he was and found regular work to do, copying little pictures for a man who sold them; and all the money he earned, he saved for the expense of his journey.

One day, when he thought that he had almost enough, he received a letter. It was from the village where his home was, but not from his mother. A neighbor wrote to him, telling him that his mother was too sick to write for herself, and that his brothers were sick, too; for there was a fever in their valley, and half the people in the village had caught it. The neighbor said that he did not think Karl's mother would die if she had good care, and that he was doing all he could for her and for the brothers, but there was no money with which to buy good food or medicines for them, and their near friends were almost as poor as they. So he had decided to write, although Karl's mother would not agree to it, asking him to come home.

It was pretty hard to receive a letter like this, when he was almost ready to finish the journey that had been so long and hard. Karl thought about it for a long time; but

of course he decided that there was but one thing to do—
he must go home where his mother needed him. He was
now not so very far away, and the money that he had saved
for the longer journey would be enough to buy a good
many comforts for the sick ones. So he bade good-by to
the man who had employed him, and took the quickest
way he could find toward home.

Although it had been a little hard to change his plans,
when Karl was once on his way home it was surprising
how happy he felt about it. He did not know how much
he had missed his mother and his brothers and the old place
until his face was turned toward them again. So instead
of feeling sad about going in that direction, he could hardly
wait to come in sight of the little village; and when he had
really arrived in it, he could not wait to get a sight of his
mother, but ran down the street as fast as his feet would
carry him until he reached the door of their little house.
Sure enough! There was his mother at the door to meet
him; for she was recovering from the fever, and through
the window had seen him running down the street.

Then Karl told her about his journey, and why he had
come home; that he had not yet found the most beautiful
sight in the world, but that he now felt more willing to
wait for it. "For," said he, "I have seen many beautiful

61

things, and I can make pictures of them. Someday I may be able to finish the journey. But I am so happy to be at home again and to see you, that I do not feel now as if I cared about anything else."

Then his mother took him by the hand, and they walked together out into the little garden, where everything was gay with the late summer flowers. "Why, dear me!" said Karl. "I never knew that we had such a beautiful little garden! Have you changed it any since I have been away?"

"No," said his mother, "but it grows a little better every year, even when left to itself."

"It is certainly the prettiest garden I ever saw," said Karl. "And look at that view of the hills behind the village! How beautiful it is with the afternoon lights and shadows lying on it! Why, mother, was that view of the hills always there just in the same way?"

"I think it must have been," said his mother, smiling at him. "You always thought it was a pretty sight, Karl."

"Yes," said Karl, "but nothing half so beautiful as this. And you too, mother, you have grown lovelier than you ever were before, in spite of your having been sick and poor. If I were a great artist, I should paint your portrait and make my fortune by it."

His mother smiled again, not believing what he said, but being pleased that he should think so.

"Mother," said Karl again, "I *will* paint your picture, sitting here in the garden, with the flowers blossoming about you and the view of the hills behind you. If I can only make it seem as beautiful to others as it does to me, it will be the best picture I have ever made."

So the next morning Karl made his mother sit in the garden, and then he brought his paints and went to work. He was afraid that everything would not look so beautiful as it had the night before, when he had first come home, but it did. He worked faster and more joyfully than he had ever worked before, hoping that he would be able to put into the picture the wonderful new beauty that he saw all around him.

At sunset the picture was almost finished, and Karl sat alone in front of it, for his mother had gone into the house to get supper. He was feeling a little tired and discouraged, as he nearly always did after a long day's work. Perhaps, he thought, it would be impossible for him to make other people see what he was seeing, and the picture would be nothing, after all, but a pleasure to his mother and himself.

"As soon as it gets too dark to work on it any longer," he said, "I shall go into the chapel to see my Angel of

63

Beauty. I am sure she will comfort me, as she always used to do."

Just then he thought he heard someone beside him, and when he looked up quickly, there stood the white Angel herself at his side, just as he had seen her so often in the chapel window! Karl was so surprised that he could not think of anything to say, but sat looking up at her with big, wondering eyes.

"I have been here helping you all day," she said, "but I thought it would comfort you more if you could see me." Then she touched his hand lightly with her hand, and Karl went to work again with his brush, which now seemed to do its work with a wonderful skill that he had never noticed in it before. "Ah," he said happily, "that was the color I wanted all the time! And that is the light on the hills that I saw last evening and thought so beautiful!"

Then, resting from his work a minute, he turned his face again toward the Angel and said to her:

"Will this really be the picture that I have wanted to paint for so long?"

"Yes," said the Angel, "it will; for at last you have found the most beautiful sight in the world."

"And it was here all the time?" said Karl.

"What is here does not make the picture," said the An-

64

gel, "but what you see." Then she faded away as quietly as she had come, and Karl saw that his picture was finished.

This was the picture that made all the world know that Karl was a great artist; but how it came to be painted has never been told before.

# The Boy Who Went out of the World

THERE was once an unhappy boy who thought that this world was not a very nice place. He was not a poor boy, for he lived with his father in a large house, and had a great many toys, and a fine garden in which to play, and all that he wanted to eat.

But, of course, as he was not thankful for all these things, they could not make him happy.

The thing about this world that the boy particularly disliked was that it was so stupidly regular. You always knew when the sun would rise and when it would set; and you knew that when it set—and sometimes even sooner—nurse would come and tell you that you must eat your supper and get ready for bed. The boy had never yet seen the time when he wanted to go to bed at the time nurse wanted him to. And it was just so about getting up, and being ready for breakfast, and being ready for school, and coming in to wash your hands in time for dinner: everything went round and round in the same way, and you could hardly ever do what you wanted to, because it was time for something else. The boy thought that on this account it was probably the worst world ever made.

Sometimes the trouble was of the opposite kind. If you wanted the sun to rise a little earlier than usual, it would never do it, and if you wanted Christmas to come in the middle of November, there was no way to manage it. So you had to wait for a great many things, and this made you impatient. It was particularly bad to have to wait to be ten years old, for the boy had been told by his father of a good many fine things he could have, and a good many other fine things that he could do, when he should be ten years old. Nothing had ever been so slow in coming as that tenth birthday, and the nearer it came—according to the calendar—the slower it was about it. The decent thing for a birthday to do would have been to come a little faster all the time, and finally, when it was only a week away, to hurry so fast that it would be there before you knew it. But it did nothing of the kind. So a week before it was to be there, the boy asked his father if he would please hurry up his birthday in some way, or, if he could not do that, would he please buy him another one that could be delivered at once. But his father shook his head and showed the boy the calendar again, and told him that birthdays could not only not be hurried, but that they actually came more slowly the more you tried to make them hurry. So that was only another proof of what a poor world this is to live in.

At last, three nights before his birthday was really to come, the boy made up his mind that he could not stand it any longer. When his nurse thought he had gone to sleep, he was out of his bed and standing at the window ledge, looking up at the stars. They shone so brightly that it seemed as if you could reach out and touch them, and the boy, remembering that each of them was a great world like this, made up his mind that if he could only get to one of them, he could certainly live there more happily than on the earth. He had never thought before that it might be possible to do this, and he was not sure now how to go about it; but he believed that his father's secretary could tell him. His father had a remarkably wise secretary, who knew a great many things that he never told, and as he studied the stars a great deal, it seemed likely that he might know how to get to them. He was not particularly fond of

68

the boy, but he was very fond of the boy's dog; and the boy thought that if he should offer to give him the dog, the secretary would tell him anything he wanted to know.

So he went very quietly through the long hall and knocked at the secretary's door.

"Come in," said the secretary.

"I want to see you about something very important," said the boy. "I am so tired of this world that I have decided to go to some other world, if I possibly can, and I thought perhaps you could show me how to get to one of the stars. If you will, you can have my dog, and anything else of mine you want, for of course I should not have any more use for them." The secretary did not say anything for a long time. Then he said:

"I suppose I could let you have my Light Magnet."

"And what is that?" asked the boy.

"It is a very strong Magnet," said the secretary, "that works with light. If you take it in your hand and hold it where a lamp can shine on it, you will be drawn across the room to the light so quickly that you hardly know what has happened, but so gently that you are not hurt at all. I have always thought that I could draw myself up to the moon or a star, if I should try; but as I never wanted to leave the earth, I have not found out surely."

"That would be fine!" cried the boy, clapping his hands;

69

and when the secretary was sure that he meant what he said, he went to his desk and took out the Light Magnet. It looked very much like a round stone, about the size of a large paperweight or inkstand, and in the center of it was a spot like a mirror, which reflected brilliantly any light that shone on it, and made it look as if it had a heart of fire.

The boy took the precious thing back to his room, and, having first put on his warm clothing and his overcoat, so that he would not be cold while traveling, he threw open the window and sat down on the ledge with his feet hanging outside. Then he turned the Magnet straight toward the star that seemed nearest and brightest, and waited impatiently to see what would happen. At first nothing happened, and the boy was afraid the secretary was mistaken in thinking that the Magnet would work with a light so far away; but in another minute he felt it giving a little tug in his hands, and when he held on to it tightly, the tug pulled at his arms and then at his whole body, and before he really knew what was happening, he had been drawn off the window ledge and was moving through the air like a bird.

At first the boy was almost frightened, when he looked down and saw the lights of his father's house and of the whole city growing dimmer underneath him; but when he looked up and saw the star seeming already to come nearer, he was glad that he was leaving the earth, and shouted "Hurrah!" to himself as he moved swiftly along.

Of course he had no way to measure time, so he could not tell how long it was before his journey ended; but it was certainly a wonderfully short time when the star stopped looking like a big light, and instead showed like a world, with the sun shining on it, and with hills and valleys and cities like the earth he had left. Then in a few minutes more the boy alighted on the ground. "Hurrah!" he said again. "Now I am in another world."

He now walked some distance before he met anyone, for it was in the open country that he had arrived. At last a man appeared coming toward him, and when they came near each other both of them politely took off their hats.

"You seem to be a stranger," said the man.

"Yes," said the boy, "I have just come from the world, and landed on your star. Did you ever meet anyone from the world before?"

"Why, this is the World," said the man. "I guess you must mean that you have come from one of the stars."

The boy did not want to be rude, so he said, "Well, I suppose it depends on how you look at it."

"And why did you come away from your star?" asked the man.

"Oh, I did not like it at all," said the boy. "For one thing, the sun rises and sets every day at about the same time, and you have to go to bed when it sets and get up when it rises; and I thought I should like to go to a world where the sun shines all the time. So I'm very glad to find it shining here, although it is night."

"But it isn't night at all," said the man. "It is the middle of the day with us. After a while the sun will set, just as it does with you."

"Bless me!" said the boy. "I'm sorry to hear that. I had no idea that it would be so in any world but ours. But there were other reasons why I didn't like our world. The years were so very long, and you couldn't have a Christmas or a birthday until just the day for it came round."

"How long were your years?" asked the man.

"Three hundred and sixty-five days," said the boy. "Don't you think that is a pretty long time?"

"Well, I don't know," said the man. "Our years are four hundred and seventy days long."

"My goodness!" said the boy. "And do you have only one birthday in a year?"

"Of course," said the man. "How could you have more?"

"I don't know," said the boy, "but I thought perhaps up

In another minute he felt it giving a little tug in his hand.

here you could have a birthday whenever you wanted it to come."

"Why, we go around the sun just the way you do," said the man, "and that is what makes years."

"And do you have to wait a long time for winter to come when you want the snow, and then another long time for the summer when you want the green grass and the flowers? I thought perhaps up here you could have summer one day and winter the next, if you happened to want it so."

The man shook his head. "I don't know just where you would find a world like that," he said. "But surely you will not find it here."

By this time the boy felt pretty much discouraged.

"Well," he said, "I think I shall have to try another world, for this one seems to be even worse than the one I came from."

So he thanked the man for all he had told him, and walked about a little more, eating, as he walked, from fruit trees that grew by the roadside. Then when he was tired he lay down and went to sleep.

When he awoke it was dark, and the stars were shining. "Now is my time," he said, "to try another world." He brought out his Light Magnet and pointed it at the star that seemed brightest, and presently he was traveling toward it as fast as he had the night before.

73

This second star proved to be a rather better-looking world than the first one, and the boy was pleased to find cold weather there, for it had been summer in the other world, and he thought it very pleasant to have winter come in the middle of summer in this way. But when he began to ask questions of the first man he met, he was disappointed again. "This is very pleasant winter weather," he said politely, "but I suppose you will soon get tired of it and have something warmer?"

"It would not do us any good to get tired of it," said the man of the second star, "for we shall not have any warm weather for about three hundred days."

"Three hundred days!" said the boy. "Why, that is almost a year."

"Oh, no, I beg your pardon," said the man of the second star, "a year is six hundred days with us."

"And you can't possibly have any summer until the time for it comes?"

"Why, how could we?"

"And you can have a birthday only once in six hundred days?"

"That is true."

"Then if I lived here," said the boy sadly, "I should not be anywhere near ten years old. Can you not tell me of any star that doesn't behave in so stupidly regular a way?"

74

"I don't think I can," said the man of the second star. "But you might try a comet. They do not behave in quite the same way that the stars do. I saw one last night that you might try if you care to."

The boy thanked him, and once more lay down to rest until nightfall. Then he saw the comet, riding in the sky with a very long tail, and turned his Light Magnet on it. Pretty soon he was going toward the comet as fast as he had gone toward the stars.

The comet did not look like the other worlds. Part of it was on fire, and the boy was frightened when he saw this; but the part on which he alighted was cool, though it seemed to be made of cinders from fires that had been burning not long before. There were no fields or cities, so far as he could see, and it did not look like a pleasant place to live in. At first, indeed, it seemed that there were no people on it, but after he had walked a long way the boy found a hermit, and the hermit asked him—as the men in the stars had done—where he had come from. Then the boy explained that he had come to the comet because he had not been able to find any other kind of world that did not go regularly around the sun, and have long, stupid seasons and years.

"Well," said the old hermit, when he had heard what

75

the boy had to say, "I'm afraid you have come to the wrong place again."

"Oh, dear!" said the boy. "You don't mean to tell me that a comet is as regular as a star. I have always heard that you never could tell when one would come in sight, or how long it would be before it would come again."

"That," said the hermit, "is only because you.could not see very far. It is true that comets travel very differently from stars, and have different seasons, and all that sort of thing. But you can be pretty sure about them if you know their habits. For instance, this comet can now be seen on the earth where you came from. But according to your way of counting time, it will be two hundred and seventy years before it has gone around its course and come back to the place where your people can see it again."

The boy's eyes grew as big as saucers, so surprised was he to hear this.

"Then your years," he said, "must be two hundred and seventy times as long as ours!"

"Yes," said the hermit. "We go through a great many different parts of the sky, and we have all kinds of seasons that you do not know anything about, and it is all very interesting. Perhaps you would like to stay on and see things for fifty or a hundred years or so. But, after all, we go just as steadily and faithfully along our own course as your world or any of the others."

"And in all the parts of the sky that you have been through," asked the boy, "have you never seen any kind of world that went where it pleased, and had no regular course of its own that it had to keep to?"

The wise hermit thought for a minute, then he shook his head. "Only broken pieces of worlds," he said, "and they soon burn up or explode."

The boy was almost ready to cry with disappointment, but he would not do so before the hermit.

"I think I will go back to my own world," he said. "It seems to be as good as any I can find. Do you think you could show me where it is, when night comes, so that I shall not make a mistake and go to one of the stars?"

"Yes," said the hermit, "I can show you tonight. But we are going so fast that in a day or two we shall soon be altogether out of sight of your world, and I do not know how you would get back to it then, except by waiting the two hundred and seventy years."

"Then I will start the first minute I can," said the boy, "for if I waited all that time, there would be no one left at home to know me, and besides I should be so old that I don't think I could make the journey."

So the moment it grew dark enough on the comet to see

77

the stars come out in the sky, the wise hermit pointed to one of them that was low on the edge of the horizon, and told the boy that that star was really his own world; and the boy, after thanking him for his kindness, turned his Magnet toward it, and was soon setting out on his journey home. As he went, he thought for the first time that it was fortunate his world did go about so regularly, otherwise he could never have told where to find it, and might have had to wander from star to star all the rest of his life.

The boy now felt some fear that he might alight at another part of the world from that in which his father lived. For all he knew, it might be the opposite side of the earth that was facing the comet. But fortunately it was not. It happened to be the very town in which he lived that he saw lying beneath him as he came dropping down out of the sky; and in fifteen minutes after he alighted, he was walking into the yard of his father's house.

The secretary came to the door to meet him.

"So you have come back?" he said.

"Yes," said the boy. "Your Magnet is a very nice thing, and I am much obliged for it; but as I could not find any other world that suited me any better than this, I have come back, and shall return your Magnet if you will give me back my dog."

"Certainly," said the secretary. "And it is very fortunate

78

that you returned just when you did. For your birthday supper is all ready for you, as everybody thought you would surely come home in time for that. If you had not been in the world before twelve o'clock tonight, when your birthday will be over, I do not see that you would ever have got to be ten years old."

"How queer!" said the boy. "I never thought of that." And, as he could now smell the birthday supper, he went directly in to eat it.

# The Palace Made by Music

*M*ANY hundreds of years ago there was a kingdom in a distant country, ruled by a good king
who was known everywhere to be rich and
powerful and great. But although the capital was a large

and beautiful city, and the king was surrounded by nobles and princes almost as rich and powerful as he, there was one very strange thing noticed by everyone who came into the kingdom: the king had no palace. He lived in a plain house near the edge of the city, not half as large or fine-looking as many of those belonging to his subjects. And he had lived there for a good many years.

Of course there was a reason why the kingdom had no palace. It had not always been so. Years before, in the reign of the present king's father, there had stood in the midst of the capital city perhaps the most beautiful palace in the world. It was a very old building— so old that no one knew when it had been built; and it was so large that, although people often tried to count the number of rooms it contained, they always grew tired before they had finished. The walls were of white marble, with splendid columns on all four sides, and behind the columns, in spaces cut into the marble walls, were pictures in bright colors that people came from distant countries to see. No one knew who had built the palace or painted the pictures on its walls; for it had been the treasure of the kings and people of the kingdom for a longer time than their history told anything about.

Then, when the present king was but a little child, the palace had been destroyed. On a festival day, when the

81

royal family and the greater part of the citizens were marching in a procession outside the city, there had come a great earthquake. All over the kingdom the people heard the rumbling and felt the ground shaking around them, but they had no idea what a terrible thing had happened, until they came to the city. Then they found that the earth had opened and swallowed up the palace in one great crash. Not so much as a single block of the marble remained. The crumbled earth fell into the opening, covering the ruins out of sight and leaving a great rough piece of ground like that in a desert, instead of the beautiful spot that had always been there in the center of the city.

Everyone felt thankful, first of all, that the king and all his family had been outside the building when the earthquake came, but in spite of this they could not help mourning deeply over the loss of the palace. The king himself was so saddened by it that he grew old much sooner than he would otherwise have done, and died not many years later. It seemed useless to try to build another palace that would satisfy those who had seen the splendor of the old one, and no one tried. When the young prince became king, although he could not remember how the palace looked in which he had been born, yet he had heard so much of its beauty that he mourned over its loss as deeply as his father, and would not allow any of his nobles or

counselors to propose such a thing as the building of a new
one. So he continued to live in the plain house near the
outskirts of the city, never going near the great empty space
in the center of the capital. And this was how he came to
be the only king in the world without a palace.

But although everyone agreed that it was useless to try
to build a new palace in the way in which other buildings
were made, there were always some who hoped for a new
one which should be no less splendid than the old. The
reason for this was a strange legend that was written in the
oldest books of the kingdom. This legend related that the
beautiful old palace had been made in a single day, not having been built at all, but having been raised up by the sound
of music. In those early days, it was said, there was music
far more wonderful than any now known. Men had forgotten about it, little by little, as they grew more interested
in other things. Indeed, everyone believed that there had
been a time when, by the sound of music, men could tame
wild beasts and make flowers bloom in desert places, and
move heavy stones and trees. But whether it was really true
that the great palace had been made in this way—this was
not so certain. There were some, however, who believed
the legend with all their hearts, and they had hopes that a
new palace might be made as beautiful as the one destroyed
by the earthquake. For, they said, what has been done can

83

be done again. If it is really true that a great musician made the old palace, it may be that someday we shall find a musician who can make another.

The musicians, of course, were especially interested in the old legend, and many a one of them made up his mind to try to equal the music of the earlier time. Often you might pass by the edge of the waste place where the old palace had stood, and see some musician playing there. He had, perhaps, been working for years on a tune which he hoped would be beautiful enough to raise a new palace from the ruins of the old. In those days men played on lyres or harps, or on flutes and pipes made of reeds that grew by the waterside; there were no organs, no orchestras and no choirs. So the musicians came alone, one by one, and played their loveliest music, not minding that those who passed by often laughed at them for believing that anything would come of it; for they did not mind being laughed at when they had hope of such great glory as the maker of a palace would surely win. This went on year by year, until the young king grew to be almost as old as his father had been when he died, but no musician as great as those of the earlier time was found.

Now there lived in the city a boy named Agathon, who wished to be a musician. He had played on the lyre ever since he was old enough to carry it, and there was no boy in the kingdom who could make sweeter music. Agathon had also a friend named Philo, who was as fond as he of playing on the lyre. They used often to talk together of the days when they should learn to play so well that they would dare to go, like the other musicians, and try to raise a new palace.

"I am sure it will be you who will finally do it," Philo would say to Agathon.

"No," the other would answer, "I shall try, but by that time I am sure you will play a great deal better than I. And if it is one of us, we are such good friends that it will not matter which."

One day the two boys made a discovery. It happened that Agathon was playing on his lyre when Philo, coming in to see him, heard the tune, and was so delighted with it that he cried, "I must try to play it, too." So he ran for his own lyre, and presently began to play before Agathon had finished. He did not strike the same notes that Agathon did, but other notes a little lower in the scale; and instead of making discord, the different notes sounded so sweetly together that both the boys looked up in surprise.

"This is a new kind of music," said Agathon, "and I think it is better than when either you or I play alone." So they tried to play in this way a number of different tunes.

When they had done this for a time they had another

85

thought. "If two different notes played together are more beautiful than one," said Philo, "why may not three be more beautiful than two?"

"Sure enough!" said Agathon. "And what is more, it may be that in this way people could make music as fine as that by which the palace was made."

Having once formed this idea, the two boys were eager that it should be tried. So they went at once to one of the chief musicians of the city with whom they were acquainted and told him what they had discovered by playing their two instruments together. Then they suggested that he should take a friend with him—or perhaps even two friends—to the place where the palace had stood, and try what could be done by the new music.

The musician was interested in what they said, but he shook his head.

"It would be of no use," he said. "There is no musician who has not tried already, and it is foolish to think that two or three of us could play together better than we can separately. Besides, each of us wants the glory of making the new palace for himself, and if we did it together no one would be satisfied."

"Would it not be enough," asked Agathon, "to have the pleasure of making it for the king, even if no one knew who had done it at all?"

"No," said the musician, "if I do it I want to do it by myself, and have the glory of it." And when the boys spoke to other musicians, they said very much the same thing.

But Agathon and Philo were not discouraged. First of all they looked for still another player; and when they heard of a crippled boy who lived not far away and who was said to be very fond of music, they asked him to join them. He was very much surprised when they told him that they wanted him to learn to play his lyre at the same time that they played theirs, and yet not to play the same notes. But presently he learned to do it, striking notes a little lower in the scale than either Agathon or Philo; and when all three made music together, they were sure it was the most beautiful sound they had ever heard.

"Let us go and play at the place of the palace!" said Philo. "It will do no harm to try."

As the next day was a holiday and they had planned nothing else to do, it was agreed. They rose very early in the morning, before any of the crowds of the city would be on the streets, took their lyres under their arms and made their way toward the place of the old palace, helping the crippled boy as they walked.

When they were near the place, they met a sad-looking man coming away. He, too, was evidently a musician, for he had a lyre under his arm. But he seemed to be a stranger in the city, and the boys stopped to ask him why he was so sad.

"I have come a long way," he said, "because I wanted to try the skill of my lyre with the musicians of your city, and see whether I could not prove myself as great a master as the one who made your lost palace. But I have tried, and have done no better than any of the rest."

"Do not be sad about it, then," said Agathon, "but turn about and try once more with us. For you have a larger lyre, with heavy strings, and I have thought that if we could add to our three kinds of notes another still farther down the scale, the music would sound more beautiful than ever. Come with us and listen when we play; then perhaps you will see how to join in and help us."

So the stranger turned about and went with the three boys to the place of the palace. Now the boys had supposed that, as it was so early in the morning, they would be the only ones there. But it happened that a great many musicians had felt, like them, that the morning of the holiday would be a very good time to make another trial of their instruments, and had also thought, like them, that by coming early they would not be interrupted by the crowds. So when the three boys and the stranger came to the street that looked into the place of the palace, they found it almost filled with musicians, some carrying lyres, like themselves,

88

They struck a great chord so much more beautiful than anything they had
ever heard before.

and some with harps or flutes or other instruments. It was all very quiet, however, since no one cared to try his skill at playing before all the rest; for every musician was jealous of the others.

After they had looked about for a few minutes and had seen why it was that so many were there and yet that there was no music, Philo said:

"Let us begin to play, Agathon. It can do no harm, and perhaps we can really show these musicians how much better music can be made by playing together than by each one playing for himself."

"Very well," said Agathon. "Let us begin."

So they took up their lyres and began to play them together as they had learned to do; and presently the stranger whom they had brought with them touched the strings of his lyre very softly, to see if he could find deep notes that would sound sweetly with those of the boys. It was not long before he did so, and when he began really to play with them, and the four lyres sounded in concert, it seemed to Agathon that he heard for the first time the music of which he had been dreaming all his life.

Now the other musicians who were standing by in silence were listening with the greatest surprise, for they had never heard any music like this in all their lives. After a little time, one and another of them, seeing that it was pos-

89

sible to play at the same time with others, took up his instrument and began to join the tune that the four were playing, for the tune itself was known to all of them, being the chief national song of the kingdom. So there spread from one musician to another the desire to take a part in this strange new music, until hardly any were left who could keep from taking up their instruments and joining in one part or another of what the others were playing. And there went up a great mingled sound that swept over the whole part of the city where they stood, and seemed to fill all the air with music. Playing in this way, all the musicians together, it happened at last that, as they grew more and more joyful with the sound, they struck a great chord, so much more beautiful than anything they had ever heard before, that they held it for a long time, not wishing to change this sound for any other, and looking at one another with eyes full of wonder and happiness.

And as they did so, there came into the volume of music the sound of great shouting, for men who had gathered in the streets to listen to the players were calling—"Look, look! The palace! the palace!" And when all the people turned their eyes to the great empty space which ·had lain waste for so long, they saw a wonderful sight. The earth was breaking away, almost as though another earthquake were pushing it, and out of the midst of it were rising great

90

walls of white marble, that lifted themselves higher and higher, until there stood in the morning sunshine a new palace of as perfect beauty as men had ever dreamed of in the old one. All these years it had waited for that great chord of music to lift it out of the earth, and at last it had come.

This, as I have heard the story, is the way in which men learned to make music together, instead of playing and singing each for himself. And this is the way in which the new palace was made for the king who had been so long without one. But no one quite knew who had done it, so the musicians forgot their jealousies of one another, and all the people rejoiced together. And if there has not been another earthquake, I suppose the new palace must be standing still.

# The Forest Full of Friends

THERE was once a little orphan girl named Elsa who lived in a lonely place by the side of a great forest with an old woman who was her only friend. Elsa's father and mother had died when she was a baby, and this old woman had brought her home to care for her, so they two had lived there together until Elsa was ten years old.

But now the old woman was growing so old that she thought it unlikely she could live much longer, so she began to look about for another place to which Elsa could go. There was only one place she could think of, and that was the king's palace. It stood in the capital city, and that was not so far away but that one could walk to it; and although the old woman had not been there for many years, she knew what a beautiful palace it was, and that it was full, not only of princes and princesses, but of courtiers and fine ladies and pages and maids-of-honor.

Now on the first day of every year the king chose from among the children of the kingdom a boy and a girl, the best-looking and best-behaved that could be found, to be kept at the palace and brought up among the pages and maids-of-honor. The old woman knew that Elsa, although she was a poor child and never had any fine clothing, was growing to be very beautiful. She was also remarkably well behaved. For these reasons, she thought, Elsa might be chosen as one of the children of the palace, and if only she were, there would be no more care about her future.

So, when the next New Year was near at hand, the old woman explained to Elsa that, as she might not live much longer, she wished to find her another home, and told her that she intended to take her to the palace in order to see whether the king would not choose her to be a maid-of-honor. Elsa was a little frightened at the thought, for she had never been in a palace, and did not believe that she could ever learn to live there. She thought it would be much more pleasant to stay with the old woman. But the old woman explained to her that that was only because she had never been to the great city and seen what a beautiful place it was. So Elsa let the old woman prepare the best dress she could find, and went with her to the city, starting very early on the morning of New Year's Day.

Elsa had never imagined anything so beautiful as the great city, with the palace standing in its center, surrounded by a splendid park. Could it be possible, she said to herself, that she would ever really live in such a place? When they approached the gate, they saw many other children coming, brought by their families and friends in the hope that they would be chosen by the king; but, though they were all dressed more finely than Elsa, the old woman said to herself that there was none of them more beautiful. So she still hoped for success.

But when they came up to the palace door and asked if they might be admitted for the choosing of the children, the porter said to Elsa:

"Where are your friends?"

"I have no friends," she answered, "except this old woman."

"Impossible!" said the porter. For he saw that she was really very beautiful, and wished to admit her. "You must have other friends. Do you not know that it is one of the rules that every child coming today must bring five friends to introduce him to the king? And the more rich and powerful they are, the better pleased the king will be."

Then Elsa and the old woman noticed that all the other

children coming through the entrance were accompanied by groups of friends, dressed quite as splendidly as the boys and girls themselves. But it did them no good to learn of this custom, for neither of them had a friend in the whole city.

"I am very sorry to have troubled you," said Elsa to the porter, "but I have no other friends in the world."

And the porter, though he spoke very kindly to them, knew that the king would not allow him to break the rules. So he opened the gate for them, and they turned sadly away.

When they reached home that night they were very tired, and the little house at the edge of the forest seemed small and lonely after the sight of the great city and its people. Still, Elsa was not sorry to be at home again, and to find that she need not leave the old woman. There was only one thing that made her sad: that was to think that she had no other friends. She had never been troubled by this before, but when she had seen the children playing together on the city streets, and had been unable to think of any friends in the whole world whom she might ask to introduce her at the palace, she knew for the first time what it was to be really lonesome. And for this reason the little yard of the old woman's house was no longer as pleasant a place as it had been before.

The old woman watched Elsa and knew why it was that

95

she was not happy. A day or two after their journey to the city she called her into the house and said to her:

"I think you had better go into the forest and play."

"Why, what do you mean?" said Elsa, for the forest was very big and dark, and people were so afraid of what might be hidden in it that throughout all the kingdom it was called the Forest Full of Fears. So Elsa said: "Why are you not afraid to have me go into the forest?"

"Because," said the old woman, "you are old enough now to know that there is nothing bad in the forest, if you take nothing bad into it. And as I see that you are feeling lonely, I think you might find some friends there."

This seemed even more strange to Elsa, that friends could be found in that great, dark forest. But she believed that the old woman must know what she was talking about, so she made ready to go.

"Come here," said the old woman again, before she had started. "I have something to give you. These are very wonderful drops that my father gave to me before he died, and I have been keeping them for you all these years, for there are not many of them left. You must use only a drop or two at a time."

"And what are they for?" asked Elsa.

"To put on your ears," said the old woman, "so that you may understand anyone who speaks in a different language

96

from your own. I think you may find some friends in the forest that you could not understand without them. So take them with you." And she gave Elsa a tiny bottle, which the little girl hid inside her dress with the greatest care. It seemed very strange to her to be really walking in the Forest Full of Fears, but she did not feel afraid. It was a bright day, so that the sunshine came through the thick branches of the trees and made beautiful shadows on the ground. There was also a little breeze blowing through the forest that made the leaves rustle in a whispering way, as if they were talking to Elsa. Indeed, the more she listened to them, the more it seemed to her as if they were really trying to speak to her.

"I wonder," she said to herself, "if the little bottle could help me to understand them?" Since it would do no harm to try, she took it out and touched each of her ears with a drop of what was in it.

Immediately a very strange thing happened. The leaves seemed to rustle just as they had before, but Elsa now knew just what they were saying. It was:

"Welcome to the Forest Full of Friends!"

"Dear me!" said Elsa. "Is that what you have been saying all along? Why, I supposed this was the Forest Full of *Fears.*"

This time the leaves said: "No, no, no, no, no!" and

97

then repeated what they had rustled before: "Welcome to the Forest Full of Friends!"

"Well," said Elsa, "if that is really its name, I am glad I came to it, for friends are the very things I want most."

She had not gone far into the forest before she heard another sound, that of a brown bird that sat singing on the branch of a tree. It did not occur to her that his song could have any particular meaning, but as she came nearer to him he did not fly away, like the birds she had seen outside the forest, but stopped his song and chirped at her as if he had something to tell her.

"Is it possible," said Elsa, "that I can understand the bird too?" She took out her little bottle again and put another tiny drop on each of her ears. Sure enough! Though the bird's voice sounded just as it had before, what he was saying was now perfectly plain. It was:

"Good morning! Good morning! It's a beautiful morning!"

"Good morning," said Elsa politely. "It *is* a lovely morning, that's true. Do you live here in the forest?"

"Yes, indeed! Yes, indeed! Yes, indeed!" said the bird. "I'm very glad to see you."

"Thank you," said Elsa. "I'm very glad to see you, too, but you must not let me interrupt your singing." For she did not quite know what else one could talk about to a bird, yet she wanted to be as polite as possible. The bird understood, and went on with another verse of his song.

Elsa walked on into the forest, now and then picking a pretty flower, and sometimes sitting down to rest on a mossy bank. While she was sitting in this way at the foot of a tree, a squirrel came down from one of the branches over her head and began chirruping merrily at her. He was a very gay little squirrel, with laughing eyes and a tail that shook when he laughed like a fat man's sides. Elsa was very sure she wanted to understand the squirrel, and indeed she found that she could do so without putting any more drops on her ears. He was saying:

"Jolly old forest, isn't it? Jolly old forest, isn't it? You've no idea where my nuts are, have you? But you're perfectly welcome to any you can find."

He seemed to think this was such a good joke that Elsa laughed, too, as she answered:

"Thank you. I *should* like a nut or two pretty soon, for my walk has made me a little hungry."

The squirrel did not make any answer, but ran up the side of the tree again, and Elsa was wondering whether she could have offended him, when a big nut fell straight into her lap. She looked up and saw the squirrel's eyes twinkling at her. Then he threw down another nut, and

99

another, until she called to him that she could not possibly eat any more.

Surely there was never a forest with more polite or more friendly people in it. After she had left the squirrel's tree, Elsa met a very pleasant little chipmunk, and a frog who lived in the brook, and a wood mouse whose home was at the roots of an oak tree, besides I do not know how many more cheerful birds. She was delighted to find that she could understand all of them, by the help of the old woman's wonderful gift; and they told her that they did not need any magical drops to help them to understand her, for they had ways of understanding boys and girls that they had known for hundreds of years. By the time it was growing dark, and Elsa began to hurry back toward home, she felt as if she had made more friends that day than in all her life before. And indeed she had.

From that time the old woman never saw her looking lonely. The forest was always close at hand, and there were always new friends to make, as well as old ones to visit with. Elsa often took crumbs of bread and cake into the forest, as gifts to her friends there, and they showed her all their secret stores, and let her take whatever she wanted, knowing that she would never really rob them or wish them any harm. So before many months had gone by, Elsa had actually forgotten that there had ever been such a place as the Forest Full of Fears.

At last nearly a whole year had passed since the old woman had taken her to the city, and Elsa remembered that it would soon be time for the king to make another choice of children for the palace. She reminded the old woman of this, and laughingly said to her:

"In those days I had no friend but you. Now I have plenty of them, if the king only knew it."

"Sure enough!" said the old woman. "I think we had better go again to the palace and tell the porter that you have a Forest Full of Friends, if he will come here to see them."

The old woman was thinking again that she had not much longer to live, and she was also very sure that Elsa had been growing more and more beautiful all the year, so she fancied that in some way they might be able to get admission to the king, and persuade him to take her as one of the children of the palace. She took out the dress which Elsa had worn the year before, and made it large enough for her to wear again. Then she told her that they would make another journey to the city on New Year's Day.

When the old woman awoke on the morning of the great day, she found Elsa already dressed for the journey, but to her astonishment she saw that the child had with her a squirrel, a bird, a frog, a butterfly and a cricket—some of them perched on her shoulder, the others in her hands.

"Why, what in the world is all this?" asked the old woman.

"These are my five friends from the forest," said Elsa. "I do not want to go to the palace again without any friends to introduce me, and so I went into the forest very early and asked them if they would be willing to go with us. And when they found the reason, they were all delighted to come."

The old woman did not quite know what to say to this, but she followed the wise rule of saying nothing in such cases. So they set out on the road to the city, with Elsa's five friends for company.

Everything in the city looked just as it had the year before: there was the same crowd entering the palace gates, and the same porter at the door. When he saw Elsa and the old woman, he remembered them at once, and he was certain that Elsa was twice as beautiful as she had been a year ago.

"But," he said, "why have you all these creatures with you? Are they presents for the king?"

"No," said Elsa, "they are the five friends that you said I must have to introduce me. Last year I had only one friend, but now I have plenty."

"Very good," said the porter. "But I do not see how these friends can introduce you to the king, when they cannot speak his language.

"If you will only let me take them in to the king," said Elsa, "I shall promise that he will understand what they say." For she had brought her little bottle along, and knew that it would do for the king what it had done for her.

At last the porter threw open the door, for although he had no idea what Elsa meant, he was sure the king would wish to see such a beautiful girl. So he led her and the old woman and the squirrel and the bird and the frog and the butterfly and the cricket to the room where the king sat on his throne.

"If your Majesty pleases," said Elsa, "I have brought five friends to introduce me, as the porter told me I must do. If you will only touch your ears with two drops from my little bottle, you will know what they are saying."

The king was so much surprised that he did not know what to answer. But Elsa was so beautiful that he thought she might perhaps be a fairy child, so he took the drops which she offered him and touched them to his two ears. Then the bird began to chirp, and the squirrel began to chatter, and the frog began to croak, and the cricket began to sing, and the butterfly flew close to the king's ear and whispered so low that no one else could have heard him, even if the room had been very still. No one but the king knew what the five friends said—not even Elsa, for she had not taken any of the drops for herself. But she was sure that her friends would say only pleasant things about her, for they all loved her dearly. The king was so much pleased to be able to understand them and to hear what they said that he beckoned to Elsa to come to him, and then drew her close and set her on his knee—a thing that no king had ever been known to do before.

"So you want to come to live in the palace, and be brought up as a maid-of-honor, or perhaps a princess?" he said.

"Yes," said Elsa, "if your Majesty wants me, and if my oldest friend, who has taken care of me all my life, can come to stay here, too, as long as she lives."

"It shall be done!" said the king. And he sent word to the porter that he need not admit any other little girls to be chosen until next New Year's Day.

So they showed Elsa and the old woman to their rooms in the palace, where they were to live happily for many a long day. But first Elsa asked leave to take her five friends to a gate in the palace wall, from which they could easily find their way back to the forest.

"Would you not like to keep some of them here with

No one but the king knew what the five friends said.

you?" asked the king. "I should really like to have them for my friends, too."

"You may easily have them for your friends," said Elsa, "but they would not be happy away from their own forest. And I do not think I can be happy, either, unless I can often go back there to visit them."

"You shall do so," said the king.

And he gave orders that the map of the kingdom should be changed, so that the Forest Full of Fears should now be known everywhere as the Forest Full of Friends.

# The Bag of Smiles

THERE was once a queer little town in a country
which has now been almost forgotten. It lay just
at the edge of an immense forest, and near green
fields and pleasant hillsides; and if you had walked through
the town you might have thought that the houses looked

very much like those in other towns, and the people living in them like the people in all the rest of the world. But you would have been mistaken. In this town there was something sadly different from any other place you could find.

The difference was that no one in the town was happy, or ever smiled. At a little distance the people looked like other people, except that they had grown very thin from never laughing; but when you came closer you saw that their faces were all exceedingly long and did not have any of the wrinkles that are made by smiling, but only those that come from worries and frowns. And at certain times of the day, such as the hour when school was dismissed and the children came out on the street, there was silence, when in other places the air was full of shouting and laughter.

The reason for all this was as strange as the thing itself. There had once been in this town a wise old woman, who, besides knowing how to take care of her garden and knit stockings, had known how to care for all the sick people in the town, and make clothes for all the poor people, and cookies for all the children, and, indeed, had known how to do almost everything that could be asked. Greatest of all, the wise old woman had learned how to be happy. She said so herself, and no one had the least doubt of it. All the other people of the town wanted to learn the wonderful secret; but whenever they would come to her and say, "Where do you get your happiness?" she would always answer:

"Why, out of the Bag of Smiles, to be sure."

But as no one had ever seen the Bag of Smiles, no one knew what it was. The people hoped that, as the wise woman grew older, she would perhaps give it to some of her friends, or perhaps leave it to them when she died, if not before. But instead of dying, the old woman had simply disappeared. One sad day she had been seeen walking into the great forest, as she often did to gather herbs, and she had never returned. Her little cottage was found in perfect order, left as if she might have been going away on a journey, and for a long time it was supposed that she would soon come back. But she never did.

Worst of all, they could find no trace of her secret, or of the Bag of Smiles. They hunted in her little house, but could find nothing in her drawers but what they had often seen there—stockings that she had knitted for the poor children, neat little packages of lavender and dried sweet clover, and herbs with which she had made medicine for the sick. After this the town grew sadder and sadder. Everyone thought, since the old woman had gone, that the secret of being happy must now be discovered over again; and the richest man in the town offered a large reward to whoever would find the Bag of Smiles. No one dared to go far into the forest to look for it, where it might be that the old woman had taken it or left it hiding, for the forest was so deep and dark that it was thought to be unsafe for travelers. But almost everyone hunted for the Bag in one way or another. The farmers stopped caring for their fields so that they might have more time for the search, and there came very near being a famine. Many of the children gave up their playing and their picnics for the same reason, and it was hard to find anyone who could do anything for you, because everybody wanted all his time to himself in order to find the secret.

But, instead of finding it, they all grew more and more unhappy. It was then that their faces began to grow long, and they began to forget how to smile even as much as they had done before. So people no longer came to the town when they heard what an unhappy place it was, and things went on in the worst possible way.

Now there was a little boy named Hilary, who lived alone with his grandfather in one of the houses nearest the forest. It happened that Hilary was not quite so sad as most of the people about him, because his grandfather was old and lame, and Hilary had to take care of him and run errands for him so much that he did not have much time to think about the things that everyone else was so anxious about. But of course he had often heard the story of the wise old woman and the lost Bag, and wondered if the time would ever come when he should be able to hunt for it. It seemed to him that it would be best to go into the forest, no matter how dark and dangerous it was, and try to find the old woman herself; for surely she must be in there, if she had never come out.

But Hilary never had any time to himself until his grandfather died. Then he was left alone, and at first he felt sad enough. He knew nothing of the world, except the sober people in the town, and the trees at the edge of the forest with their whispering leaves and the little birds that sang in the branches, and of the two he preferred the trees. Then there came to him the thought that now he was free to hunt for the wise old woman, and learn the secret of the Bag of Smiles. If he could only find it and share it with all the people in the town, what a different town it would be!

So, without waiting for the neighbors who were coming to take him to live with them, Hilary went softly about his grandfather's house and gathered up in a handkerchief all the things that he wanted to take with him. There were nuts and buns for his luncheon; a compass to help him on his journey; a sling, in case he should meet any giants or wild animals in the forest; and one or two little things that had been his grandfather's, to remember him by. With only this bundle, and his everyday clothes and cap, Hilary started into the forest, not telling anyone of his plans. When the neighbors came to the cottage they found it empty; and as no one had disappeared so strangely since the time when the wise old woman had gone away, some said that perhaps she had come out of the forest and taken Hilary, because he had been left alone.

In this way the boy began a long journey, never knowing to what place he was coming, or indeed how far he had traveled from home; but it did not matter, since he never cared to go back. The forest, even if it was big and dark, he still found more pleasant than the town full of dreary people. It was not until sunset that he began to feel lonely and to wish for some cozy place where he might sleep. But so far there was no sign of a clearing or of any kind of house. Hilary was hurrying along, hoping that at least he might find a hollow tree in which to go to sleep, when he heard something say "Chee!" in a mournful little voice.

He looked everywhere, and at last saw a bird at the foot of an elm tree. It had evidently met with some accident and broken its wing, for it could lie only on one side, rolling its round eyes and saying, "Chee!" as though it would ask for help.

"Dear me!" said Hilary. "I am very sorry for you, but I don't think I can stop now, as it is almost dark and I am looking for a place to sleep. Perhaps your wing will be better in the morning."

"Chee-weep!" said the little bird.

"Dear me!" said Hilary again. "It is pretty bad to be alone in the forest with a broken wing. I believe I shall have to stop and help you, after all."

So he sat down at the foot of the tree, picked up a twig and began to make a splint for the wing, such as he had seen his grandfather make for a hurt pigeon. Then he tore a bit from his handkerchief with which to fasten the splint, while all the time the little bird rolled its eyes and tried to thank him as well as it could. At last Hilary had done all that he knew how to do, and said good-by to the bird, so that he could hurry on his journey again; but now the bird called after him so loudly that he could not help turning back. Then he saw that it had started to hop along the ground, and even to fly a few feet at a time. It was not following Hilary, but going off in another direction, and seemed to be calling to Hilary to follow. When the boy came closer, the bird moved on a little farther, still calling; and at last it occurred to Hilary that perhaps his new friend was trying to lead him to a place where it had a nest.

"Who knows," he said to himself, "but it might be a good place for me to make my nest, too, since I can find no house." And he began to follow the little bird willingly.

Soon after this it grew dark, but the bird kept calling, so that Hilary could still follow it through the forest. And at last something happened: he saw a light ahead. Almost at the same minute he noticed that the little bird had stopped calling; in fact, it had flown into the low branch of a tree and put its head under its wing, ready for a night's sleep. So Hilary had only to go on toward the light and see if he could find shelter.

The light was from a big house that stood in a big clearing in the forest, and when Hilary knocked at the gate he was met by a kind housekeeper, who was very glad to let him come in and to find a place for him to spend the night. Then he discovered that this was the house of a very rich man, who had so much gold and silver that he did not know what to do with it. He had been so much troubled by the people who came to ask for his money that he had moved here to the forest, where he lived alone with his servants and his little girl.

"Now," said Hilary to himself, "if he has lived here a long time, perhaps he can tell me something about the old woman I am looking for, or, at any rate, about the Bag of Smiles."

So in the morning, when he saw the rich man walking

113

in the garden that surrounded the big house, he went to him and asked if he could give him any help in his search. But the rich man said that he had never heard of the old woman, and that, although he had heard of the Bag of Smiles, he had never seen it, and doubted whether there really was any such thing. And as for knowing the secret of being happy, he was far too busy taking care of his gold and silver to have any time for that.

So Hilary, after thanking him for his night's rest and for the good breakfast that the housekeeper had given him, was ready to go on his journey again. But just at that moment one of the servants came up and told the rich man that his little daughter Phyllis was lost. She had gone into the forest for her morning walk, and it seemed that she had been chasing a butterfly until she had got a long way from her nurse, and when the nurse had gone to look for her, she was nowhere to be found.

Then the rich man began to be greatly frightened, and gave orders that the servants should stop all their other work and go into the forest to look for Phyllis. And Hilary, seeing how distressed he was, offered to help also.

"If I could only meet with my little bird again," he said to himself as he started off, "I should not wonder if he would help me find the lost Phyllis, as he helped me to find the house in the clearing."

And he had no sooner thought this than he heard something say "Chee!" Sure enough, there was the little bird hopping along in front of him. It could fly better this morning than on the night before, but never flew so far that Hilary could not easily keep up with it, and went on into the forest as if it knew just where it was going. Hilary did not know whether it would really do him any good to follow the bird, but since he had no idea of his own as to the way to go, he was sure that at least it could do no harm; so on he went, wherever his little friend led him among the trees.

At last, after a long, long walk, he saw something ahead of him that looked like gold; and when he came nearer it proved to be the hair of little Phyllis, as she lay on the grass where she had gone to sleep, after she had discovered that she was lost. So Hilary came close to her and awakened her by speaking her name softly. Then he took her by the hand and led her back, the little bird still showing the way, to her father's house.

When the rich man saw that Hilary had found his little daughter, he was so pleased that he invited him to stay at his house as long as he liked. But Hilary thanked him and told him that he must go on his journey to hunt for the Bag of Smiles. "And if I ever find it," he said, "I shall come back again and let you share it."

So after he had taken luncheon with the rich man and Phyllis, he started on his way again into the forest. It was now afternoon, and of course he had no idea how far he must go before nightfall in order to find another good resting place; but the little bird still went with him, and Hilary felt sure that it would lead him by a good path. The forest was as dark and thick as it had been the day before, but it no longer seemed so lonely, and sunset came again before he realized it. Still the little bird led him on through the wood, until at last he saw another light ahead, and knew that they must be near another house.

Again Hilary knocked at the gate, and a kind porter let him in and said he would be very glad to entertain him. This was another big house in another big clearing, and Hilary learned that it was the house of a very great man, who had been so famous that all the people in the world wanted to come and look at him; and to get away from them he had come into the great forest, as the rich man had done, and lived alone with his servants and his little boy. Hilary thought it very likely indeed that the great man would know something about the old woman and the Bag of Smiles, but the man told him the same thing that the rich man had told him. "And," said he, "if you wish ever to be a great man like me, I advise you to give up looking for it, for I doubt very much if it will ever be found."

So on the next morning Hilary was preparing to go on his journey again when a strange thing happened. He heard the servants making a commotion about something, and when he inquired if there was any trouble, they told him that the great man's little boy was lost in the forest.

"How very odd," said Hilary. "I wonder if somebody is lost in the forest every day." Then he told them that he knew a little bird which could find any lost person, and he would go with the bird and try to bring back the little boy, as he had brought back Phyllis on the day before. And they were very glad to have him do so.

The little bird led the way to where the lost boy was playing in the woods, and did so even more quickly than he had found the lost Phyllis, for he was now able to fly almost as well as ever, and Hilary would run after him with his nimble legs. So they brought the little boy back to his father, and although he, too, was so grateful that he invited them to stop at his house, they excused themselves and again started on their journey.

Now on the third night the little bird brought Hilary to a third house in a third clearing, where he found the people quite as kind as he had in the other two places. It happened that this was the house of a very wise man, who had been so much troubled by the people who came from all over the world to ask for his wise advice that he had finally come to the forest, like the rich man and the great man, and built him a house where he could live quietly among his books. He had no family except a dwarf whom he kept to bring him his books and brush the dust off them.

"Surely," said Hilary, "this wise man will be more likely to know about the Bag of Smiles than anyone I have found yet."

But he was disappointed again. For the wise man was even more certain than the rich man and the great man that it was foolish to expect to find such a Bag. And as for learning how to be happy, "I shall perhaps begin to try to find out," he said, "when I have finished reading all the books in my library; but I doubt very much if that time will ever come."

When Hilary was ready to leave the wise man's house on the next morning, he said to himself: "Well, this time I shall really have a whole day in which to look for the old woman, for the wise man has no little boy or girl to get lost in the forest."

But the strange thing was that he was mistaken. He had already gone a long distance from the clearing when he heard someone running after him. It was one of the wise man's servants, who had been sent to ask Hilary if he had seen anything of the dwarf.

"No, indeed," said Hilary. "Is he lost?"

"No one can find him," said the servant, "and we thought he might have gone away with you."

"Well," said Hilary, "if he is in the forest, my little bird can find him; and of course we will try, since the wise man has been so kind as to entertain me."

Now the dwarf had grown tired of carrying and dusting the wise man's books, and had thought he would run away for a day and have a vacation. But he was already growing lonesome when Hilary and the bird found him, and was glad to return with them; for it was not at all certain that he could find his way back alone. And the wise man was as thankful to have his dwarf back again as the rich man and the great man had been to find their children.

When Hilary set out again on his journey, he had a new idea. He and the little bird had found so much pleasure in hunting the lost people in the forest, that he began to think he did not care to give it up.

"This is evidently a very bad forest to travel in," he said to the little bird, "unless you have someone to show you the way. And people are getting lost in it all the time, for there must be a great many others living here that we have not yet seen. Let us stay in the forest, and, instead of hunting any longer for the Bag of Smiles, since everybody tells us that we shall never find it, let us hunt for lost people, and mark little paths where they can go about without losing their way."

The little bird said "Chee!" as though he thought the idea a very good one, and Hilary felt happier over his new plan than he had ever felt in his life.

But he must have some place to live while in the forest, and he wondered where it would be. So he said to the bird:

"See if you cannot find a nice little house for us, near the part of the forest where it is thickest and darkest, and where the most people are likely to be lost. It will not matter if it is empty, we shall soon learn to take care of ourselves."

Then the little bird spread its wings and flew so fast that Hilary had all he could do to keep up with it. He followed it until the trees grew so close together that he could hardly find a path, and it was so dark that he could hardly tell whether the sky was blue. On and on they went, until at last they came to a little clearing with a little house in the middle of it, and the bird flew to the top of the house and perched on the gable of the roof.

Hilary went up to the door, and tapped, so as to find whether anyone lived there. And the door was opened by the most delightful old woman that you could ever think of, with a white cap on her head, and her face full of little

Then the little bird spread its wings and flew so fast that Hilary had all he could do to keep up with it.

wrinkles such as are made by smiles. She had her knitting work in one hand, and with the other she held the door open while she said "Good evening" to Hilary.

Hilary's eyes had grown wider and wider as he looked at her; and at last he said:

"Why, I believe you must be the wise old woman with the Bag of Smiles!"

Then he told her how he had left the town where she had once lived to hunt for her and her Bag, and how the little bird had led him from one place to another through the forest, and how at last he had made up his mind to give up hunting for the Bag, since everyone told him that it could not be found, and instead to find a house in the forest and become a guide for people who had lost their way.

"Well," said the old woman, "so you have been making friends with my bird, and trotting about with him all these days that he has been away from home?"

"Your bird!" said Hilary. "Why, if it was your bird, why did he not show me the way to your house in the first place?"

"Because," said the old woman, "he never brings anyone to my house who is looking for it. Do you think that is strange? I have nothing to give anybody, and only this poor little house that you see."

"Then it is not true," asked Hilary, "that you have the Bag of Smiles?"

The old woman laughed a pleasant laugh. "Perhaps I may have it," she said, "but I never saw it. I am sure, if I have, that you must have it, too, for you were smiling as hard as you could when you told me about the way in which you and my bird have been helping people out of the forest, and how you have enjoyed it."

"And do you agree with me," said Hilary, "that that is a better thing to do than to go on hunting the Bag?"

"Of course I do," said the old woman, "and so does the bird, or he would never have brought you here. If you want to stay here and live with us, we shall be very glad to have you. My porridge is cooking now, and we can soon have supper."

So Hilary, who thought that nothing in the world would be nicer than to stay in such a dear little house with such a delightful old woman and such a friendly bird, went in and laid down his bundle. And when the old woman served the porridge for supper, the little bird flew in at the window and sang to them while they ate.

# The Castle under the Sea

THERE was once an island kingdom in a distant ocean, whose people were all boatmen and fishermen. They lived entirely apart from the rest of the world, and were glad to remain by themselves. Indeed there would never have been a happier place, if it had not been for one thing. They had an enemy who was about as bad an enemy as one could easily imagine; and nothing that the king or any of his counselors could do succeeded in making them less afraid of him.

This enemy was a wicked Water Prince, who had magical powers, and lived in a great castle at the bottom of the sea. He hated the people of the island kingdom, for no other reason than that he hated all good people and good things. He had done them harm in many ways, for as long a time as anyone could remember, by taking the fishes that they needed for food, although he had no use for them at all, and by raising many large and cruel fish of other kinds, which not only devoured the good fish, but would attack the people of the kingdom whenever they had opportunity.

Many times the king had sent the best of his subjects to fight the Water Prince, and some of them had made their way to the place under the sea where his great castle stood; for the people of the kingdom had lived by the ocean so many hundreds of years that they could breathe under the water as well as the fishes, and knew the plants and animals that lived on the bottom of the sea almost as well as they did those on shore. But, in spite of all this, no one had ever been able to find a way to enter the castle, even if he had been brave enough to do it, or to think of any way in which to destroy it.

Worst of all, the Water Prince had now made a prisoner of the king's son. The king's son was only a young boy, but he was eager to grow up so that he might fight against his father's enemy, and he had said so many times that when he was a man he knew he should succeed in destroying the magic castle and driving the Water Prince away, that the Prince came to be afraid that it was true. So one day when the boy, whose name was Valma, was out in a boat with some of his companions, the Water Prince sent a great fish to overturn the boat, and then, though he let all the other boys escape, he himself seized Valma and carried him off to his castle.

This nearly broke the heart of the king of the island kingdom, and he offered great rewards to anyone who should rescue his son from the magic castle. But no one dared even try, for the Water Prince had sent word that Valma was now alive and safe in his castle, but that he would put him to death as soon as any of the king's men came to rescue him. So the king mourned many months, and all his people with him; and many gave up hope that Valma would ever see his home again.

Now there lived not far from the king's palace a little girl named Milna, whose father was gardener of the palace gardens. She was a happy child, spending most of her time out in the fields or along the water's edge. She loved every living thing so much that the birds and squirrels and fishes returned her love, and would come to her whenever she had food for them, or wished to play with them. Although her father was a poor man, and she did not have many fine clothes or other things that only money could

125

buy, yet there was perhaps no girl in the island kingdom who was loved by so many people, or who had so many friends.

One day the gardener, Milna's father, was very much surprised to receive a visit from the Chief Wise Man of the king, who was thought by most people to know more than any other man in the world. The gardener bowed very low to him and asked him why he had honored him by coming to see him.

"I wanted to speak with you about your daughter," said the Chief Wise Man.

The gardener could not think why the people in the palace should have any interest in his daughter, and he was very sure she could not have been doing anything wrong of which they could complain. So he asked:

"Are you sure you mean my daughter, Milna?"

"Yes," said the Chief Wise Man. "I have heard many good things of your daughter, and I have three questions to ask you about her."

"Very well," said the gardener.

"Did you ever know her to be unkind to anyone?"

The gardener thought a moment. "No," he said, "I am sure I never did. I do not think you could find a man who has seen her unkind to any living thing."

"Very well," said the Chief Wise Man. "The second

126

question is: Did you ever know her to speak anything but the truth?"

The gardener could answer this without stopping to think. "No, indeed," he said. "I do not think Milna has ever even thought of such a thing as an untruth, or would know what it is."

"Very well," said the Chief Wise Man. "The third question is: Did you ever know her to be afraid of anything?"

The gardener thought a little about this. Then he said: "No, I never knew her to be afraid, because she has always trusted everyone as she has been trusted by them. But, of course, she is only a girl."

"Very well," said the Chief Wise Man again. "I do not care if she is only a girl. I think that she can rescue the king's son if you will let her try."

Then the gardener was startled indeed. "Rescue the king's son!" he cried. "When she is only a little girl, and none of your soldiers or counselors has been able to do it!"

"It is not like other things," said the Chief Wise Man. "The Water Prince, as you know, has magical powers, and he cannot be conquered by those who are strong or who have good swords. I have been studying in my secret books ever since Valma was taken captive, to find who it is to be who should rescue him. And lately I found the answer: It is to be one who has never been unkind, or untruthful, or

127

afraid. And your daughter is the only one in the kingdom of whom anyone has said the three things as you have said them to me."

They talked a long time about it, and at first the gardener could not bear to think of his little girl going to rescue the captive of the great and wicked Water Prince; but when the Chief Wise Man showed him that it was his duty to his king to give all that he had to save Valma, he gave his consent.

"But," said he, "while I am sure that Milna cannot be unkind or untruthful, I am not sure that she cannot be afraid. I should be afraid, myself, if I were asked to go against the Water Prince."

"Very well," said the Chief Wise Man. "We can easily find out about that by asking her to go. If she is afraid, we do not want her."

So Milna was called in from the garden, and the Chief Wise Man took her by the hand, and, without telling her any of the things that he had said to her father, he asked her if she would like to help rescue the king's son. Now of course Milna knew all about the king's son; and she had not only thought about his capture, but had often wished she were a man, instead of a girl, so that she might help restore him to his father. She answered at once:

128

When Milna saw him she almost shouted for joy.  Then she came close to him
and spoke his name.

"I should like it very much indeed, if there were any-thing I could do."

"But," said her father, "would you not be afraid, since he is a captive of the wicked Water Prince?"

"No," said Milna, "I do not think I should, for I am not big or important enough for the Water Prince to care to hurt me. And besides, if I were really trying to rescue the king's son, I should be so happy about it that I should never think of being afraid."

The Chief Wise Man now felt sure that he had found the one whom he had been seeking, and he asked Milna if she would be ready to start the next morning for the castle under the sea.

"Yes," said Milna, "but what am I to do when I find it?"

"That I cannot tell you," said the Chief Wise Man, "for all that my secret books tell me is that you are the one who can rescue the king's son. So I think you will know for yourself, when the time comes, what you have to do. Go to the castle, find Valma, and bring him back with you—that is all."

"Quite enough, I should think," said Milna's father, "seeing it is what all the rest of the kingdom has been un-able to do." But secretly he was becoming glad that such a great mission was given to his little daughter.

Early the next morning the Chief Wise Man came again

129

to the gardener's house, and he and Milna and the gardener went together down to the seashore. Milna wore her sea-water clothing, and, when she had bidden her father and the Chief Wise Man good-by, she walked into the sea and was soon lost to sight.

"It is really a little queer," she thought, as she went along the bottom of the ocean, farther and farther from the island, "that I am not afraid to go off in this way all alone. Yet, after all, why should I be afraid? I have often walked here with my father, and the fishes are fond of me, and it is such a beautiful place that I can never be lonesome."

So she walked on among the beautiful ferns and trees that grow on the bottom of the sea, and the fishes who were friendly to her followed her wherever she went, eating the crumbs that she had brought for them in her pocket. The Chief Wise Man had told her in which direction to walk to find the castle of the Water Prince, and it turned out that the distance to it was not so great as she had supposed.

Now there were three gates to the castle under the sea. The first was made of huge rocks, brought there by the giant spirits who served the Water Prince. The second was of coral, made to order for the Prince, and still unfinished, although it had been building for a hundred years. The third gate, like the castle of which it was a part, was made of nothing but sea water, and was of the color of a soap bubble with the sun shining on it. It was held together by magic, and if anyone tried to come near it, it moved away as if it were not really there but had only been dreamed.

When Milna came to the first gate, she found it guarded by two of the giants that served the Water Prince. If she had really seen how big these giants were, she might have been frightened, after all. But they towered so far above her head that she only saw part of their legs among the rocks of which the gate was built; and as she was not looking for giants, but only for the way through the gate, she paid no attention to them. For just the same reason the giants did not notice Milna, since she was so near the bottom of the sea, and their heads were so high above it, and as the gate was open, she went through it without stopping to ask anyone's leave.

The second gate was also guarded by giants, and as they were seated at the foot of the great archway, they saw her approaching. One of them spoke to her.

"Who are you?" he asked. "And why are you seeking to pass through this gate?"

"I am on my way to the castle under the sea," said Milna.

"And why do you want to go to the castle?"

"To see Valma," she answered, "who is the son of the king of my country."

131

Now the giants had seen many people from the island kingdom who had tried to come near the castle of the Water Spirit, but none of these people had ever really told what they had come for. Instead, they had made up a hundred different tales to try to deceive the guards at the gate. But it had never occurred to Milna to tell anything but the truth when the giants questioned her, and they were quite taken by surprise. Indeed they felt so sure that Milna could not possibly mean what she said, that they supposed she had not really come to try to enter the castle at all, but was only amusing herself by what she told them. So they laughed at her answer, and, since she was quite too little to be considered an enemy of the Water Prince, they did not hinder her from passing through the second gate.

So Milna now passed on toward the castle itself, which she could already see rising before her. It was the most wonderful sight she had ever seen, as it towered high into the upper ocean, with walls and towers and turreted gateways, all floating and trembling and glimmering like the walls of a soap bubble. From a little distance it seemed that you could easily look clear through the walls, but this was only an appearance. No one had ever discovered what was inside, or had been able to guess how the castle was really made. But the Chief Wise Man of the island kingdom had read in his secret books that there was just one sort of person who could have power over the castle under the sea, and that was one who had never done an unkindness. So it was for this reason, although he had no idea what Milna would do when she reached the place, that he had asked her to go.

Milna herself did not know any of these things. She was still wondering how she could ever rescue the prince, even if she should finally enter the castle and find him; but the Chief Wise Man had told her that she would know all she needed when the time came. So she walked straight up to the castle gate, thankful that there seemed to be no guards there to keep her out. For this gate had no need of any guards, and the Water Prince himself, who was looking from a window of the castle, laughed when he saw the little girl approaching. He guessed that his giants had let her pass through the outer gates because they were so sure that she could do no harm, and he made ready to enjoy the sight of her surprise when she tried to touch the castle and found that she could not do so.

But the Water Prince never saw what he was waiting for. A wonderful thing happened. When Milna lifted her hand and knocked on the great gate of the castle, the gate suddenly broke like a bubble, and instantly all the towers and walls behind it broke in the same way. They might have melted into drops of water and mingled with the sea,

133

or they might have vanished into nothing at all. Whichever it was, before Milna could catch her breath in surprise, the castle was gone. She looked all around for it, but nothing could be seen except a great stretch of green sea water, like that through which she had come.

And the Water Prince, trembling with fear when he saw that here was the only one, of all who had ever come into his dominions, who had power to destroy his magic castle, fled so fast that never a bit of him showed to Milna's eyes.

She walked over the spot where the castle had been a minute before, wondering if it had all been a dream. Had Valma gone with the castle, so that he could never be found, after all? No; he lay sleeping under a great water plant whose branches drooped over his head. The destruction of the castle had been so silent that it had not made him stir in his sleep. When Milna saw him she almost shouted for joy. Then she came close to him and spoke his name. He opened his eyes dreamily.

"Why, where is the castle?" he said. "And the Water Prince? And all his servants who have kept me prisoner?"

"I do not know," said Milna, "but they are gone. I am sent by the king, your father, to bring you home with me."

So Valma rose gladly, and took Milna's hand in his, and they made their way back toward the island with no one to hinder them, for all the servants of the wicked Water Prince had fled, like him, when they saw that the castle had been destroyed.

The king and the Chief Wise Man and the other wise men and the gardener and many of Milna's friends were waiting on the shore for her return. When she came dripping out of the water, and they saw that she had Valma, the king's son, by the hand, they gave such a shout that the Water Prince himself must have heard it, though by this time he was hundreds of miles away.

# In The Great Walled Country

AWAY at the northern end of the world, farther than men have ever gone with their ships or their sleds, and where most people suppose that there is nothing but ice and snow, is a land full of children, called

The Great Walled Country. This name is given because all around the country is a great wall, hundreds of feet thick and hundreds of feet high. It is made of ice, and never melts, winter or summer; and of course it is for this reason that more people have not discovered the place.

The land, as I said, is filled with children, for nobody who lives there ever grows up. The king and the queen, the princes and the courtiers, may be as old as you please, but they are children for all that. They play a great deal of the time with dolls and tin soldiers, and every night at seven o'clock have a bowl of bread and milk and go to bed. But they make excellent rulers, and the other children are well pleased with the government.

There are all sorts of curious things about the way they live in The Great Walled Country, but this story is only of their Christmas season. One can imagine what a fine thing their Christmas must be, so near the North Pole, with ice and snow everywhere; but this is not all. Grandfather Christmas lives just on the north side of the country, so that his house leans against the great wall and would tip over if it were not for its support. Grandfather Christmas is his name in The Great Walled Country; no doubt we should call him Santa Claus here. At any rate, he is the same person, and, best of all the children in the world, he loves the children behind the great wall of ice.

137

One very pleasant thing about having Grandfather Christmas for a neighbor is that in The Great Walled Country they never have to buy their Christmas presents. Every year, on the day before Christmas, before he makes up his bundles for the rest of the world, Grandfather Christmas goes into a great forest of Christmas trees that grows just back of the palace of the king of The Great Walled Country, and fills the trees with candy and books and toys and all sorts of good things. So when night comes, all the children wrap up snugly, while the children in all other lands are waiting in their beds, and go to the forest to gather gifts for their friends. Each one goes by himself, so that none of his friends can see what he has gathered; and no one ever thinks of such a thing as taking a present for himself. The forest is so big that there is room for everyone to wander about without meeting the people from whom he has secrets, and there are always enough nice things to go around.

So Christmas time is a great holiday in that land, as it is in all the best places in the world. They have been celebrating it in this way for hundreds of years, and since Grandfather Christmas does not seem to grow old any faster than the children, they will probably do so for hundreds of years to come.

But there was once a time, so many years ago that they

138

would have forgotten all about it if the story were not written in their Big Book and read to them every year, when the children in The Great Walled Country had a very strange Christmas. There came a visitor to the land. He was an old man, and was the first stranger for very many years who had succeeded in getting over the wall. He looked so wise, and was so much interested in what he saw and heard, that the king invited him to the palace, and he was treated with every possible honor.

When this old man had inquired about their Christmas celebration, and was told how they carried it on every year, he listened gravely, and then, looking wiser than ever, he said to the king:

"That is all very well, but I should think that children who have Grandfather Christmas for a neighbor could find a better and easier way. You tell me that you all go out on Christmas Eve to gather presents to give to one another the next morning. Why take so much trouble, and act in such a roundabout way? Why not go out together, and everyone get his own presents? That would save the trouble of dividing them again, and everyone would be better satisfied, for he could pick out just what he wanted for himself. No one can tell what you want as well as you can."

This seemed to the king a very wise saying, and he called all his courtiers and counselors about him to hear it. The wise stranger talked further about his plan, and when he had finished they all agreed that they had been very foolish never to have thought of this simple way of getting their Christmas gifts.

"If we do this," they said, "no one can ever complain of what he has, or wish that someone had taken more pains to find what he wanted. We will make a proclamation, and always after this follow the new plan."

So the proclamation was made, and the plan seemed as wise to the children of the country as it had to the king and the counselors. Everyone had at some time been a little disappointed with his Christmas gifts; now there would be no danger of that.

On Christmas Eve they always had a meeting at the palace, and sang carols until the time for going to the forest. When the clock struck ten everyone said, "I wish you a Merry Christmas!" to the person nearest him, and then they separated to go their ways to the forest. On this particular night it seemed to the king that the music was not quite so merry as usual, and that when the children spoke to one another their eyes did not shine as gladly as he had noticed them in other years; but there could be no good reason for this, since everyone was expecting a better time than usual. So he thought no more of it.

There was only one person at the palace that night who

was not pleased with the new proclamation about the Christmas gifts. This was a little boy named Inge, who lived not far from the palace with his sister. Now his sister was a cripple, and had to sit all day looking out of the window from her chair; and Inge took care of her, and tried to make her life happy from morning till night. He had always gone to the forest on Christmas Eve and returned with his arms and pockets loaded with pretty things for his sister, which would keep her amused all the coming year. And although she was not able to go after presents for her brother, he did not mind that at all, especially as he had other friends who never forgot to divide their good things with him.

But now, said Inge to himself, what would his sister do? For the king had ordered that no one should gather any presents except for himself, or any more than he could carry away at once. All of Inge's friends were busy planning what they would pick for themselves, but the poor crippled child could not go a step toward the forest. After thinking about it a long time, Inge decided that it would not be wrong if, instead of taking gifts for himself, he took them altogether for his sister. This he would be very glad to do; for what did a boy who could run about and play in the snow care for presents, compared with a little girl who could only sit still and watch others having a good

141

time? Inge did not ask the advice of anyone, for he was a little afraid others would tell him he must not do it; but he silently made up his mind not to obey the proclamation.

And now the chimes had struck ten, and the children were making their way toward the forest in starlight that was so bright that it almost showed their shadows on the sparkling snow. As soon as they came to the edge of the forest, they separated, each one going by himself in the old way, though now there was really no reason why they should have secrets from one another.

Ten minutes later, if you had been in the forest, you might have seen the children standing in dismay with tears on their faces, and exclaiming that there had never been such a Christmas Eve before. For as they looked eagerly about them to the low-bending branches of the evergreen trees, they saw nothing hanging from them that could not be seen every day in the year. High and low they searched, wandering farther into the forest than ever before, lest Grandfather Christmas might have chosen a new place this year for hanging his presents; but still no presents appeared. The king called his counselors about him and asked them if they knew whether anything of this kind had happened before, but they could tell him nothing. So no one could guess whether Grandfather Christmas had forgotten them, or whether some dreadful accident had kept him away.

As the children were trooping out of the forest, after hours of weary searching, some of them came upon little Inge, who carried over his shoulder a bag that seemed to be full to overflowing. When he saw them looking at him, he cried:

"Are they not beautiful things? I think Grandfather Christmas was never so good to us before."

"Why, what do you mean?" cried the children. "There are no presents in the forest."

"No presents!" said Inge. "I have my bag full of them." But he did not offer to show them, because he did not want the children to see that they were all for his little sister instead of for himself.

Then the children begged him to tell them in what part of the forest he had found his presents, and he turned back and pointed them to the place where he had been. "I left many more behind than I brought away," he said. "There they are! I can see some of the things shining on the trees even from here."

But when the children followed his footprints in the snow to the place where he had been, they still saw nothing on the trees, and thought that Inge must be walking in his sleep, and dreaming that he had found presents. Perhaps he had filled his bag with the cones from the evergreen trees.

143

On Christmas Day there was sadness all through The Great Walled Country. But those who came to the house of Inge and his sister saw plenty of books and dolls and beautiful toys piled up about the little cripple's chair; and when they asked where these things came from, they were told, "Why, from the Christmas-tree forest." And they shook their heads, not knowing what it could mean.

The king held a council in the palace and appointed a committee of his most faithful courtiers to visit Grandfather Christmas and see if they could find what was the matter. In a day or two more the committee set out on their journey. They had very hard work to climb the great wall of ice that lay between their country and the place where Grandfather Christmas lived, but at last they reached the top. And when they came to the other side of the wall, they were looking down into the top of his chimney. It was not hard to go down this chimney into the house, and when they reached the bottom of it they found themselves in the very room where Grandfather Christmas lay sound asleep.

It was hard enough to waken him, for he always slept one hundred days after his Christmas work was over, and it was only by turning the hands of the clock around two hundred times that the committee could do anything. When the clock had struck twelve times two hundred hours, Grandfather Christmas thought it was time for his nap to be over, and he sat up in bed, rubbing his eyes.

"Oh, sir!" cried the prince who was in charge of the committee, "we have come from the king of The Great Walled Country, who has sent us to ask why you forgot us this Christmas, and left no presents in the forest."

"No presents!" said Grandfather Christmas. "I never forget anything. The presents were there. You did not see them, that's all."

But the children told him that they had searched long and carefully, and in the whole forest there had not been found a thing that could be called a Christmas gift.

"Indeed!" said Grandfather Christmas. "And did little Inge, the boy with the crippled sister, find none?"

Then the committee was silent, for they had heard of the gifts at Inge's house, and did not know what to say about them.

"You had better go home," said Grandfather Christmas, who now began to realize that he had been awakened too soon, "and let me finish my nap. The presents were there, but they were never intended for children who were looking only for themselves. I am not surprised that you could not see them. Remember that not everything that wise travelers tell you is wise." And he turned over and went to sleep again.

145

The committee returned silently to The Great Walled Country, and told the king what they had heard. The king did not tell all the children of the land what Grandfather Christmas had said, but, when the next December came, he made another proclamation, bidding everyone to seek gifts for others, in the old way, in the Christmas-tree forest. So that is what they have been doing ever since; and in order that they may not forget what happened, in case anyone should ever ask for another change, they have read to them every year from their Big Book the story of the time when they had no Christmas gifts.

DL